# THE DEATH RIDERS

# THE DEATH RIDERS

Jackson Cole



Chivers Press
Bath, England

G.K. Hall & Co.
Thorndike, Maine USA

This Large Print edition is published by Chivers Press, England, and by G.K. Hall & Co., USA.

Published in 1999 in the U.K. by arrangement with Golden West Literary Agency.

Published in 1999 in the U.S. by arrangement with Golden West Literary Agency.

U.K. Hardcover ISBN 0–7540–3651–0 (Chivers Large Print)
U.K. Softcover ISBN 0–7540–3652–9 (Camden Large Print)
U.S. Softcover ISBN 0–7838–0445–8 (Nightingale Series Edition)



The text of this Large Print edition is unabridged.
Other aspects of the book may vary from the original edition.

Set in 16 pt. New Times Roman.

Printed in Great Britain on acid-free paper.

**British Library Cataloguing in Publication Data available**

**Library of Congress Cataloging-in-Publication Data**

Cole, Jackson.
The death riders : a Jim Hatfield Texas Ranger western / by Jackson Cole.
p. cm.
ISBN 0–7838–0445–8 (lg. print : sc : alk. paper)
1. Large type books. I. Title.
[PS3505.O2685D42 1999]
813'.54—dc21 98–48522

## Chapter One

# THE LONE WOLF

A red moon hung over the Rio Grande. In its baleful rays the Great River was a stream of sluggish blood flowing between banks of jet. Far to the north-west the Guadalupes loomed massively against a blue-black sky silver-spangled with stars, a mighty fortress of the half-gods built to withstand the assaults of titans in the days when there were giants in the land and the half-gods made war on men. Nearer, to the west, were jagged broken hills standing north-eastward and fanging far to the south, slashing the desert with their iron claws.

East and west stretched the desert, a purple mystery flecked with silver-ash, whispering and murmuring in the wind as sand particle nestled against sand particle or caressed the weird spires of chimney rocks and buttes with tireless finger, carving the iron-hard granite into grotesque shapes and patterns. Cholla cactuses stood gaunt and menacing, brandishing twisted, deformed arms like truculent devils. Mesquite thickets, grease-wood, sage, with here and there a grove of cottonwoods where a spring welled forth from the thirsty sands and fed a little stream that soon lost itself in the reaches of parched desolation.

Edging the grey garment of the desert with emerald and amethyst was the rangeland, stretching north beyond the skyline like the waves of a sea, frozen at the crest of their swell.

And above all the vast inverted bowl of the sky with its countless stars and a red, red moon looking down with a bloody eye.

Faint with distance sounded the mournful, beautiful plaint of a hunting wolf. A weird, whickering cry answered the call from where an owl perched on the topmost limb of a blasted pine. Then for a long time the sharp edge of the silence was blunted only by the eerie whisper of the wind-drifted sands.

Gradually another sound became apparent, a muffled rhythmic clicking that steadily increased in volume. It swelled to a systematic patter, a monotonous thudding—pouring along the grey ribbon of a trail that writhed out of the west, flanked by mesquite and chimney rock, with the ash and purple vastness of the desert to the south and the distant swell of the rangeland on the north.

Around a bend in the moon-drenched trail flickered shadows. They resolved into mounted men, a full dozen or more of them, who swept eastward, riding with loose rein, glancing neither to right nor left, hatbrims drawn low, faces muffled in handkerchiefs looped high about their throats. The ghastly horsemen bulged past a shoulder of chimney rock and vanished around a second bend perhaps five hundred yards distant from where they had burst into view. The thudding died to a patter, a clicking, a whisper scarce louder than that of the sands, and ceased.

Again the silence was unbroken; but not for long. A clicking different from the multiple beat of more than twoscore hoofs vibrated the air. Like the first, it grew in volume, but at a slower rate. Another moment and a lone rider appeared, looming gigantic in the deceptive light that shimmered to reddish bronze the coat of the magnificent golden sorrel he bestrode. Lounging easily in the saddle, he rode past the bulge of chimney rock and towards the second bend in the trail.

But unlike the speeding group that preceded him, he continually glanced right and left, searched the trail ahead with a probing gaze, turned to look over his shoulder. As he neared the bend, his glance concentrated on the black curve of mesquite which walled it in. Abruptly he stiffened in the saddle, muscles tensed for dynamic action.

And at that instant, reddish flame gushed from the dense bristle of growth at the bend. The report of a shot rang like thunder and echoed back and forth from spire to butte.

The tall rider of the golden horse, who had been swaying sideways the instant the gun cracked, threw up both hands and pitched from the saddle, to lie, apparently a limp and lifeless form, undiscernible in the black shadow that edged the trail.

But even as he fell, seemingly helpless, one sinewy hand jerked a heavy Winchester rifle from the saddle boot. As he hit the ground he shot a low-voiced command to the horse:

'Hold it, Goldy!'

The yellow horse stood motionless, ears pricked forward inquiringly. His rider lay, apparently, where he had fallen. In reality, he had writhed sideways several feet farther into the shadow.

For long minutes the tableau held. The golden horse continued to peer towards the bend in the trail. From the shadows beside him came no sound or motion. The horse flicked his tail, and pawed questioningly with a front foot.

'Steady!' cautioned an almost inaudible whisper from the shadows. 'Steady, feller; that dry-gulching sidewinder will be coming to see if he did a finish job, or my name's not Jim Hatfield! Steady!'

The horse remained motionless, the silence unbroken. The sullen moon climbed higher into the sky, the band of shadow beside the trail narrowed.

It was the faint snap of a breaking twig that warned Hatfield of danger from an unexpected quarter. He glanced quickly over his shoulder and saw two shadow forms just emerging from the mesquite behind him. Noiselessly he writhed about, cuddling the stock of the Winchester against his cheek.

The two forms advanced stealthily towards him. He could catch the glint of moonlight on the guns they held. He shifted the muzzle of the rifle to bear directly on the leading figure. But just as his finger began tightening on the trigger, a vagrant beam of moonlight fell full on the face of the leading man and what he saw so startled Hatfield that for an instant he held his fire.

The moonlight, reddish, eerie, beat not upon a human face, but upon a fleshless skull—cavernous eye-holes, grinning teeth, noseless cavity! It was a grisly death's-head that topped the tall and broad-shouldered form that advanced with furtive but purposeful step.

But if the thing that stole towards him was featureless, it certainly was not voiceless. For at that moment it let out a warning bellow:

'Look out! He ain't dead!'

Jerked out of his trance of astonishment, Hatfield fired. He saw the death's-head reel back, heard his yell of pain that was healthily human. A wild dive sideways and the two forms vanished in the growth. Hatfield sent a stream of lead hissing after them, and was rewarded by a wild crashing as the pair tore through the mesquite in headlong flight.

Hatfield leaped to his feet, scudded along

through the shadow, and paused where the smashed branches showed where the pair had taken to cover. He could see nothing, but his ears told him that both of the dry-gulchers were on their feet and hightailing it away from there.

Abruptly the sound ceased. Hatfield crouched low, rifle at the ready, peering and listening. Another moment of silence, then to his ear came the sound of fast hoofs fading into the distance.

Hatfield debated whether to mount and race in pursuit, but that ominous bend in the trail ahead made him hesitate. He had no way of knowing whether the grim pair he had seen were the whole of the dry-gulching pack. If others were holed up beyond the bend, he stood a good chance of leaning against the hot end of a bullet if he rounded it recklessly. On noiseless feet he turned and stole back the way he had come, keeping in the shadow, careful to avoid the slightest sound.

He reached the bend, slipped into the growth and wormed his way along, stopping every moment or two to peer and listen. The silence remained unbroken save for the chirp of a sleepy bird in the growth ahead. A moment later the furtive form of a rodent slid across the trail a dozen yards in front and vanished into the mesquite.

'That feller wouldn't have gone in there if anybody was holed up in the brush,' Hatfield told himself. He straightened up and stepped boldly on to the moonlit trail. Nothing happened. Mechanically he refilled the magazine of his rifle with fresh cartridges. For a moment he stood staring eastward.

'The same thing saved him that saved me a minute before—moonlight glinting on my rifle barrel when I shifted it,' he mused, apropos of the vanished dry-gulcher. 'If I hadn't seen that mite of a gleam at the edge of the brush ahead, he'd have drilled me dead center. Came mighty close as it was—I felt the wind of the slug as it went past. Well, this is a nice reception for a gent ridin' into a section peaceable like! What sort of a jigger was that I lined sights with, anyhow? Looked like something that had just climbed out of a grave after spending a long time there! Captain McDowell wrote me funny things were happening hereabouts and would stand a little Ranger investigating, but it looks like he doesn't know the half of it. Looks like I might be in for a sorta interesting time.'

Most folks might reason that what had just occurred was a mite too interesting for comfort, but there was a pleased expression in the long green eyes of the man a grim old Lieutenant of Rangers had named the Lone Wolf.

## CHAPTER TWO

# FIERY DEATH

Hatfield covered perhaps a mile, riding at a swift easy pace. The moon was almost to the zenith now and had lost some of its reddish hue. But still the hot haze shrouded the sky and the light filtering through it was eerie and unreal.

The mesquite that flanked the trail was thinning somewhat. Abruptly it fell back for some hundreds of yards and Hatfield had a clear view ahead. Suddenly he uttered an exclamation.

A reddish, flickering glow was climbing up the eastern sky a little to the north of the trail. An instant later he heard, thin with distance, like the crackling of thorns under a pot, a stutter of shots.

'Now what?' he muttered, peering at the angry sky. The glow was growing more fiery. It flickered and wavered, climbed higher. Hatfield spoke to his horse.

'Something off color going on over there, or I'm a heap mistook,' he muttered. 'Trail, Goldy!'

The sorrel lengthened his stride. The rhythmic beat of his irons quickened. Hatfield leaned forward in the saddle, alert and watchful.

The mesquite was crawling back towards the trail which had veered to the north, away from the desert. Soon it crowded close, a dark bristle rising above the head of the mounted man. He could catch only occasional glimpses of the sky ahead in which the fiery glow persisted.

The trail began to curve in a gradual sweep that veered it more and more to the north. The mesquite growth thinned to a straggle, then ceased altogether. Goldy flickered past the last tangled bush, and ahead was open rangeland, softened and mellowed by the flooding moonlight. And set a few hundred yards to the side of the trail and perhaps a half mile ahead was a ranchhouse, a barn and other buildings. The roof of the barn was a mass of flames and the whole lower portion of the ranchhouse was shrouded in fire that shot angry tongues through rolling clouds of smoke.

Hatfield leaned forward tensely, spoke urgently to the racing horse, who increased his speed even more. That something was very wrong ahead was apparent, for Hatfield could make out two motionless forms lying on the ground near the door of the bunkhouse, while a third figure ran aimlessly about in the fierce glow of the fire and waved frantic and futile arms.

His horse a lather of sweat and blowing foam through flaring, reddened nostrils, Jim Hatfield pounded up to the burning buildings. He flung himself from the saddle and ran to the wild-eyed old man who was skipping about as close to the burning ranchhouse as the fierce heat would allow.

'What's going on here, old-timer?' the Ranger demanded.

'The boss!' yammered the oldster. 'He's up there on the second floor! He sleeps there! Didn't come down!'

Hatfield stared at the reddened second-story windows.

'You sure?' he exclaimed.

'Of co'hse I'm shore!' the oldster wailed. 'I saw him go upstairs at bedtime. He ain't down here now. Must be up there. He'll be burned up.'

Hatfield ran his eye over the burning house. He noted the tall chimney at one end, the top of which extended some six feet above the roof of the building. Directly opposite the chimney, about twenty feet from the house, stood a single tree.

The Ranger estimated the distance from the tree to the chimney top. He whirled and ran back to his horse, unlooped his sixty-foot rope and returned. His sinewy hand began twirling a widening loop. With all the strength of his right arm he made the throw.

The rope snaked upward towards the chimney, uncoiling smoothly, the loop wide and free. The loop barely settled over the chimney top. Instantly the Lone Wolf jerked it taut.

'Blazes, what a throw!' gasped the old man.

Without commenting, Hatfield hurried to the tree. He wound the free end of the rope about the trunk, drew the length as taut as he was able and tied it securely. He turned to the old man.

'An axe,' he ordered, 'get me an axe! Hustle. The fire's climbing up the wall fast.'

The oldster obeyed, stumping to the bunkhouse as fast as his rheumatic legs would permit. He came stumbling back almost immediately, blowing and panting, a broad-bladed axe gripped in his gnarled hand.

Hatfield took the tool and thrust the haft under his broad leather belt. He had already discarded his guns and heavy double cartridge belts. Now he gripped the taut slanting rope and began going up it hand over hand.

The old man, divining his purpose, yelled frantic protest:

'Yuh'll get caught up there! The rope'll burn through and yuh can't get down!'

Hatfield made no reply; he was saving all his breath for the climb up the steeply slanting rope. Another moment and he was close to the building. He gasped from the heat of the flames roaring up towards him, and climbed madly. He reached the eaves, wormed and twisted along until he could grasp the edge of the chimney with one hand. By a prodigious effort he scrambled on to the slanting surface, braced himself against the chimney, jerked the axe from his belt and began swinging it on the shingles. Splinters flew, the old wood crumbled and split. Soon he had an opening through the roof.

But the space between the boards to which the shingles were nailed was not wide enough to admit his body, and the wood was thick and tough. With all his strength he hacked and hewed, while the flames below roared upward, drawing ever close to the thin line of manila that was his only means of descending safely to the ground.

Finally, after what seemed an age, the tough plank was cut and smashed enough to permit his worming through the opening. A moment later and he dropped to the floor of the attic, close to the eaves.

Here the air was stifling and reeking with smoke. Hatfield groped about until he located the stairs to the second story. He stumbled down them, shoved open a door at the foot and found himself in a bedroom.

Flames were already flickering through the burning floor, and by their light the Ranger saw that he was the room's sole occupant.

Over to one side was a tumbled bed that looked like somebody had risen from it hastily, throwing the covers back in wild confusion. Nearby was a chair over which hung a pair of breeches, a shirt and overalls. A hat rested on a bedpost. Dangling from the post, under the hat, was a gun belt with the butt of a six protruding from the holster. At the foot of the bed stood a pair of well-worn boots.

His face bleak, Hatfield crossed the room to the door, which stood ajar. He peered into a hallway dimly lighted by the flames that were coming through the floor. The end door, which doubtless opened on to the stairs, was closed. Across the hall was another door, and farther along it, two more on each side.

Hatfield flung open one door after another. All the rooms were untenanted. Below he could hear the flames roaring and crackling. The air was thick with smoke, the heat almost unbearable. He raced to the end door and placed his ear against it.

'Won't do to open it,' he muttered. 'There's a regular inferno down below. From the looks of that bed and the clothes scattered about, the pore devil jumped up and tried to get out without taking time to dress. Smoke musta got him on the way down. Guess he's a goner.'

He hurried back to the bedroom. Outside the house, the old man was yelling wildly. Hatfield staggered up the stairs to the attic, gasping for breath, his head spinning, his chest feeling as if an iron band was slowly tightening about it. He groped through the smoke to the opening in the roof. It was above his head and beyond arm's reach. Crouching low, he leaped with all his strength. His clutching fingers just grazed the splintered board and he floundered back in a heap.

For an instant he lay gasping. His strength was going, and he knew there was little time to spare. Gathering himself together, he made a frantic effort to reach the opening. One hand clutched the edge of the board and for a moment he hung by the very tips of his slipping fingers. Then he got a hold with the other hand and levered his body through the opening and on to the sloping roof.

The air outside, though hot and smoky, was infinitely better than the blistering reek within the attic. Hatfield breathed great gulps of it. Dimly he heard the voice of the old man, above the roar of the flames.

'The rope's scorchin'!' he was bellowing. 'She'll burn through any minute!'

Hatfield realized his danger. He edged around the chimney, gripped the rope with both hands and swung off the roof. Flames were licking clear to the eaves now, and he gasped as they bit at his feet and legs. The rope felt like a red-hot wire to his hands, and he could smell it burning. He nearly lost his grip and dropped into the welter of flames beneath him as his hand touched a spot that was already smouldering.

At racing speed he went down the rope. He was still some twenty feet above the ground when he felt the twine slacken. Down he plunged, still gripping the burned-through rope. He struck the ground on his feet, his knees bent to minimize the shock. It was very severe, however, and knocked him clean off his feet. For a moment everything went black before his eyes. Then, as he felt the old man's hands tugging at him, he sat up, head whirling, red flashes storming before his eyes. With the oldster's assistance he got shakily to his feet and stumbled farther back from the burning building.

'Nobody up there,' he responded to the other's question. 'Clothes there, and the bed looked like somebody had just jumped out of it. I'm scairt he tried to get out too late and was trapped. There were clothes on a chair, boots beside the bed and a hat and a gun-belt on a post.'

'He allus hung his gun and hat on the bedpost,' the oldster muttered. 'Reckon he's a goner.'

'I'm afraid so,' Hatfield admitted.

The old man stared dazedly at the burning building.

'Everybody gone!' he muttered. 'Pore Hank and Billy dead, Wun-Wun, the old Chink cook, quit and left day before yesterday, the boss cashed in. Nobody left but me, and them new hands, what don't count.'

Hatfield laid a soothing hand on his shoulder.

'Easy, old-timer,' he comforted. 'How did all this happen? Who did it?'

'Them damn Death Riders, who else!' the old man exploded. 'They did it. They set fire to the house and drilled pore Hank and Billy when they run outa the bunkhouse.'

'But why?' Hatfield asked.

'To get the money, that's why!'

'The money? What money?'

'The money in the safe in the livin' room—twenty thousand dollars. The boss brung it in this afternoon and put it there—the money he got for the big herd the boys druv up to the Circle J. They'd oughta be there by now, if they didn't make camp for the night. Old Banks Buster, who owns the Circle J, has a contract with the railroad construction camps to s'ply them with meat. He's been buyin' up beefs all around and givin' good prices. The Boss just about cleaned the Runnin' W to get that herd together. He was up to the Circle J and collected, seein' as the herd was on the way. Brung the money back with him. Was gonna take it to the bank to-morrow. Them skull-faced hellions musta got wind of it somehow. That's the way they allus operate: set fire to a buildin' and shoot the fellers down when they run out, half asleep, to see about the fire. They'd have got me, too, but I snuk off to town after everybody else had gone to bed, to get me a bottle. I was ridin' back when I heard the shootin' and saw the fire. They was gone when I got here. My name's Stiffy Jones, and I been workin' for the Runnin' W for twenty years.'

Hatfield listened quietly to the half-incoherent babble of the old fellow whose nerves had evidently just about reached the breaking-point. He patted him on the shoulder, and asked a question:

'Who are the Death Riders?'

'Nobody seems to know for shore,' replied old Stiffy. 'They been raisin' hell and shovin' a chunk under a corner hereabout for the past six months. Been robbin' and murderin' and holdin' up stages and runnin' off cows. They ain't got no faces—just skull bones where faces oughta be. They got folks scairt.'

'Sounds sorta reasonable they would have,' Hatfield admitted.

Old Stiffy jumped and yelped as a crackle of shots sounded inside the burning ranchhouse. Hatfield restrained him as he started to dash away.

'The fire's got to that gun on the bedpost on the second floor,' he explained. 'That was the cartridges going off from the heat.'

Stiffy wiped his damp brow with the back of his hand.

'Thought for a minute the hellions was comin' back to finish us off,' he quavered. 'It would be like 'em to do that!'

Hatfield fished the makin's from his shirt pocket and rolled a cigarette with the slim fingers of his left hand. He proffered the brain tablet to Stiffy and rolled another for himself. For some moments he smoked thoughtfully, regarding the doomed ranchhouse, through the roof of which the flames were now spouting. The barn had already burned down to a skeleton of blazing beams and timbers. A moment later the whole mass fell in with a deafening crash, which was echoed almost instantly by the collapsing roof of the ranchhouse.

'No horses in the barn?' Hatfield questioned.

'No, thank God,' Stiffy replied. 'All the boys didn't use are in the pasture over by the other side of the grove.'

'Well, there's nothing we can do right now,' Hatfield commented. 'After the ashes cool we'll see if we can find enough bones left of yore boss for a funeral. Pity the kitchen had to go and burn down, too. I could stand a s'roundin' of chuck and a cup of steaming coffee right now. Haven't eaten for so long my stomach is asking if my throat's growed shut.'

'I've starved, too,' Stiffy admitted, the natural cravings of the outdoor man of action asserting themselves despite the presence of grim tragedy. 'Lucky there's some s'plies in the storeroom over there beyond the bunkhouse, and I reckon we got enough fire handy to cook 'em. There'll be some pots and pans there, too. I'll get 'em if yuh'll rake enough fire together out here where we can work.'

First, however, they placed the half-clothed bodies of the two murdered waddies under the tree and covered them with blankets. Then they turned to the preparation of their meal.

Both were old campaigners and half an hour later they squatted over bacon and eggs, flapjacks and cups of fragrant coffee.

'I feel better,' Stiffy announced, as he drained the last drop from his cup and straightened up with a sigh. 'Nothin' like a belly linin' to set a man up when things have been goin' wrong. Now what?'

Hatfield glanced at the sky, which was becoming overcast.

'I'm going to pound my ear for a spell,' he said. 'All we can do is wait for that fire to burn down. I've a notion we'll have rain before daylight, and that'll cool the ashes in a jiffy. Then we'll see what's what.'

It was full morning when Hatfield awoke. A slow rain was falling steadily. Ranchhouse and barn were a blackened ruin, cold and charred. He awakened old Stiffy, who was snoring on a bunk across the room.

'We got an unpleasant job to do, and we might as well get it over,' the Ranger said.

Stiffy rubbed the sleep from his eyes, procured tools, and they set to work with picks and shovels, burrowing into the tangle of blistered beams and scorched foundations. They had toiled for perhaps an hour at their grisly task when Stiffy suddenly let out a yelp.

'Bones!' he yammered, 'I see 'im!'

Hatfield nodded, and prodded carefully with his shovel. Soon they had unearthed a badly burned skeleton. A sickening stench arose from the ashes that caused Stiffy to gulp and gag.

Last to come to view was the skull of the cremated man. It had become detached from the spinal column, doubtless because of some blow from a falling beam, and lay a foot or two distant from the rest of the pathetic heap. Stiffy drew away from it in horror, but Hatfield picked it up and examined it carefully. As he did so, his black brows drew together until the concentration furrow was deep between them. He raised his eyes and stared towards the low hills to the north, dimly seen through the drifting rain mists. Then he turned and gazed down at old Stiffy Jones from his great height.

'Stiffy, what sort of a man was yore boss?' he asked.

'A fine big, upstandin' feller,' Stiffy replied. 'Big and tall, with black whiskers and snappin' black eyes. Uh-huh, Burns Wright was a fine lookin' feller.'

Hatfield nodded, and turned the scorched skull over in his hands. He examined the remainder of the skeleton with great care.

'Get a blanket from the bunkhouse,' he ordered at length.

When the blanket was forthcoming, he piled the remains upon it, refraining from asking the shrinking old cowboy to assist in the task. Then he wrapped the blanket carefully about them and carried the bulky bundle away from the ruins and gently placed it under a tree.

'Yuh can see about burying them when the rest of the outfit shows up,' he told Stiffy. 'Fust the sheriff and coroner of the county must be notified. They'll want to hold an inquest, I figger.'

Stiffy nodded dully.

'It'll be a sad homecomin' for Miss Teri—she's due at Creston, the railroad town ten miles to the east, tomorrer,' he said.

'Miss Teri?'

'Uh-huh, Miss Teri Wright. She's the real owner of the spread. Burns Wright was jest runnin' it for her till she showed up. She's been away at school all winter.'

'Burns Wright was her father?'

'Nope, her uncle. Her father was old Caleb Wright, who got himself did in by wideloopers last fall—the fust feller did in by the Death Riders, folks think, but they ain't shore. Burns Wright allus figgered the Death Riders did for him. Burns had come here from over Arizona way a coupla months before and was workin' for his brother. He took charge when old Cale took the big jump. Miss Teri was at school when Cale was cashed in. She come home for the funeral, but went back to school afterward. She was doin' her last year there and she said her Dad allus had his heart set on her graduatin', so she left her Uncle Burns to run the outfit and went back to school. And now this hadda happen right when she was comin' home to stay. Pore gal!'

Hatfield nodded sympathetically. He returned to the ruins and shifted beams and timbers until he had uncovered a ponderous iron safe that stood in what had been a corner of the living-room. The door stood open, and the inner compartments had been smashed. He examined combination knob and tumblers carefully, his brows drawing together in thought, an inscrutable expression in his long green eyes. He was just straightening up from the task when a clatter of hoofs sounded and a horseman bulged out of the straggle of trees to the east. He was a young fellow in cowhand garb, his eyes wild, his face haggard; his hatless head was wrapped in a bloody rag.

'The herd!' he yelled to Stiffy as he flung himself from his reeking saddle. 'Widelooped in Skeleton Canyon! Two of the boys cashed in! The others rode to town to get the sheriff! I come to tell the boss! What the hell's been goin' on here?'

Stiffy told him, profanely. The cowboy stared dazedly about and raised a shaking hand to his bloody face.

Hatfield took him by the arm and gently led him towards the bunkhouse.

'Come on and lie down. I'll take a look at that head,' the Lone Wolf told him. 'Stiffy, get some coffee hot.'

While Stiffy got a fire going and heated the coffee, Hatfield removed the blood-soaked rag and examined the puncher's wound. It proved to be a ragged furrow at the hairline above his left temple. He probed the skull bone with sensitive fingers.

'Just creased, nothing busted,' was his diagnosis. 'I'll wash it and tie it up. I got a roll of bandage and some salve in my saddlebag.'

He procured the bandage and medicant from the shed behind the tool house where he had made Goldy comfortable the night before. With deft fingers he cared for the wound. Stiffy brought in hot coffee and after a cup and a cigarette the young puncher recovered his composure somewhat.

'We was bedded down in Skeleton Canyon,' he replied to Hatfield's questioning. 'The Boss told us not to run the fat off them critters, so we took it easy and decided not to try to make the Circle J last night. It was just before daylight and rainin' hard when all hell bruk loose. Them skull-faced hellions downed the two nighthawks and shot up the camp. Then they stampeded the herd up the canyon. By the time we got ourselves shook together and started after them, they was plumb outa sight and hearin'. We follered 'em for a spell, but us fellers is sorta new to this section, and I reckon they know every hole and side canyon up there. Anyhow, we lost the trail. Decided we'd better hightail back for help. Yuh figger it was the same outfit burned the ranchhouse?'

'Part of the same outfit, I reckon,' growled Stiffy.

'How far to Skeleton Canyon?' Hatfield asked.

'About twenty miles,' Stiffy replied.

'It was quite a bit before midnight when they hit here,' the Ranger said. 'They woulda had plenty of time to get there and pull the widelooping just before daybreak.'

'Reckon that's so,' Stiffy admitted. 'Yuh shore it was the Death Riders, Kirby?'

'Sure for certain,' Kirby replied. 'I got a glimpse of the feller what give me the crease. He shot a coupla times before he hit me. I saw his face, or where his face had oughta been, by the flash of his gun. It weren't no face—jest skull bones and holes for eyes.'

Hatfield stared curiously at the young fellow. His hands were shaking and his face was beaded with sweat. He undoubtedly believed that he had looked upon some inhuman monstrosity. Hatfield had already arrived at his own explanation of the grisly phenomenon, but he refrained from comment for the moment.

'We'll rustle some breakfast, and then I reckon you and me had better ride to town and notify the sheriff's office what's happened here,' he told Stiffy. 'This feller can stay here and look after things till somebody shows up.'

East of the Running W spread the country changed to a long range of low hills with rounded crests. The trail wound around the giant shoulder of the range, with a steep slope swelling upward to the hilltops. Below the trail the slope continued to the desert floor, rocky and precipitous, cluttered with boulders and rock fragments and grown with tall brush. At its base ran the east-west line of the C & P railroad.

Creston proved to be a bustling cowtown, its main street lined with saloons, dancehalls and gambling houses. There was a big general store and a number of other shops. The railroad passed through it and there was a stage station adjoining the depot.

They found an elderly deputy in charge of the sheriff's office.

'Bush rode to Skeleton Canyon a couple hours back with yore hands,' he told the old Running W puncher. 'What's on *yore* mind, Stiffy?'

Old Stiffy told him. The deputy swore profusely at the news.

'I don't know what this section's coming to,' he declared querulously. ''Pears nobody is safe any more. I tell yuh things are plumb outa hand. We won't get 'em under control again till we get a troop of Rangers sent here. All Mack Bush does is chase hisself around in circles. Mack's a good man, but he ain't heavy enough to buck them damn Death Riders. I've done told him so. Other folks are of the same mind. Letters has been sent already to Captain Bill McDowell over to Ranger headquarters, askin' for help, but nobody's heard anythin' from

McDowell so far. I'm scairt he's got too much on his hands right now to send a troop over here. The Rangers have lots of territory to cover.'

'That's so,' agreed Stiffy. 'McDowell is liable to ask what we got a sheriff here for and how it's a matter for local authorities to take care of.'

'Mebbe it is,' grunted the deputy, 'but I'll tell yuh as one of them there local authorities, it ain't bein' took care of. Who's yore friend, Stiffy?'

Old Stiffy looked blank. 'Well, what do yuh know about that!' he said. 'I clean forgot to ask him.'

The deputy stared. Hatfield smiled, his teeth flashing white and even in his bronzed face. He supplied his name and shook hands with the deputy, who admitted Trout Mason was his handle.

'Let's go tell Doc Beard what happened,' Mason suggested. 'Doc Beard is coroner,' he added for Hatfield's edification.

'Yuh didn't see any of them hellions what set fire to the ranchhouse?' he asked Stiffy Jones as they set out for the doctor's office.

'Nope,' Stiffy replied, 'but I'd be willin' to swear they had skull bones for faces, and that a big tall jigger on a black horse was headin' 'em, per usual!'

Hatfield glanced sharply at the old cowhand, but refrained from comment.

As they turned in at the doctor's office, a tall, very good-looking young man was just coming down the steps. He had dark brown eyes and hair, straight features and a determined-looking chin. His right arm was in the sleeve of his coat, but the left sleeve flapped empty and the coat was draped over his left shoulder. His left arm was suspended in a sling across his broad breast. He nodded shortly to the deputy but did not speak. Trout Mason grunted, but said nothing. His eyes were hard as they followed the young man across the street to the hitchrack opposite the doctor's office. Once there, the man with the injured arm somewhat clumsily unhitched a splendid black gelding, mounted and rode up the street without a backward glance.

With another grunt the deputy led the way into the office. A white-haired old fellow with a deeply lined face, bright blue eyes and a snowy beard looked up from a table as they entered.

'Howdy, Doc,' greeted the deputy. 'What was the matter with Tom Wyman? See he had one arm in a sling.'

'Leaned against a passin' bullet,' the doctor grunted in reply. 'Said he was ridin' along the Mescalero Trail last night and somebody slung lead at him outa the dark.'

'I reckon there's several somebodies would like to do that,' growled the deputy. 'Meet Jim Hatfield, Doc. Him and Stiffy have somethin' to tell yuh.'

Old Doc Beard gravely shook hands with the tall Ranger. His face did not move a muscle, but there was a gleam in his blue eyes.

Doc listened without comment to Stiffy Jones' garrulous account of the tragedy at the Running W ranchhouse. Only after the old waddie had finished his story did he break silence.

'Stiffy,' he said, 'I can tell from the look in yore eye that yuh're plumb dyin' to get out and get a drink. Go ahead and get yore snort. This young feller can stay here and put me straight while I write out what happened for my records. Go ahead, I won't need yuh.'

Old Stiffy grabbed the opportunity with alacrity. Together with the deputy he hurried from the office.

'See yuh at the Dust Layer, jest a coupla doors down the street,' he told Hatfield as he vanished through the doorway.

When Doc Beard was sure that both Stiffy and Mason were well on their way, he turned to Hatfield with a broad grin, and for the second time extended his hand.

'Put 'er there, Jim,' he said. 'Was wonderin' how long it would be before yuh showed up. All hell is bustin' loose in this section and I figgered, seein' as McDowell has his hands full along the border and wouldn't hardly have a troop to send, that mighty soon the Lone Wolf would drop in to straighten out this mess.

How's everythin' over to Ranger headquarters? McDowell as cantankerous as ever and still bellerin'? Shore is good to see yuh.'

Hatfield shook hands again, a twinkle in his steady eyes.

'So yuh got run outa the Pecos country, eh?' he remarked. 'Somebody must a took a dose of yore medicine by mistake. Was it fatal?'

'Folks was gettin' so dadgummed healthy over there I was bein' arrested for vagrancy reg'lar the fust of each month,' the old frontier doctor replied. 'I'm gettin' rich over here—makin' almost as much money as the undertaker who's doin' the big business hereabouts, pertickler since the Death Riders have been operatin' in this section.'

'Who are the Death Riders, Doc?' Hatfield asked, his tone suddenly grave.

'Plumb bad owlhoot outfit,' Doctor Beard replied. 'Folks say they ain't got no faces, just skulls without meat on 'em.'

'An old trick,' Hatfield replied. 'White paint on black masks, that's all. Wouldn't think sensible folks would be taken in by such hocus-pocus.'

'Don't reckon they're all taken in by it, but when most everybody who gets a look at the hellions either cashes in or gets punctured by hot lead, yuh can't blame 'em for bein' sorta jumpy,' Doc replied. 'Reckon some people, pertickler the *peons* in the villages and other ignorant folks, are sorta superstitious about it. I've a notion old Stiffy Jones believes it's plumb gospel. Anyhow, they're *muy malo hombres* and they've been kickin' up plenty of merry hell hereabouts for the past few months.'

'Terror tactics,' Hatfield mused. 'Get everybody jumpy, and cash in on it. Soon, no matter what happens in a section, folks attribute it to the outfit wearing a distinctive brand. Which makes it easy for every side-trail bunch to pull things and get away with it.'

'That's right,' Doc admitted. 'Things are boomin' in this section. The railroad is buildin' south to Mexico, there's a big silver strike in the hills to the north, and this town is the shippin' and receivin' point for everythin'. All of that nacherly booms the cattle business, and this is cattle country.'

'And all of which makes fat pickings for an owlhoot outfit that's salty and has brains,' Hatfield commented. 'What about the sheriff, Doc?'

'Honest and dumb,' Beard grunted. 'Makes a good turnkey at the calaboose, and that's about all. Trout Mason, the chief deputy, ain't so bad, but he's old and sorta stove up by the years.'

Hatfield nodded. 'And what about that young feller yuh just treated for a punctured arm?' he asked suddenly.

'Tom Wyman? He owns a small spread to

the southwest of here—where the range shoots out a tongue of good land inter the desert. He just got out of the penitentiary.'

'Good place to get out of,' Hatfield commented. 'What was he sent up for?'

'Burns Wright and some of the Runnin' W hands caught him beside a fire last year,' Doc replied. 'There was a hot iron in the fire and a Runnin' W calf close by with a half-run brand on it. Jury found him guilty and the judge give him a year.'

'Not over much evidence to convict a feller of cinch-ringing,' Hatfield remarked.

'Yeah, reckon that's what the judge thought, seein' as he only give him a year. Wyman had been in trouble before, though. He had a ruckus with Burns Wright not long before that and gunned him. He's a hot-headed young cuss and had had run-ins with other folks and got hisself a reputation for bein' salty. Them things count against a jigger when he comes up for a wring with the law. Wyman did nine months—three off for good behavior.'

'How'd yuh say he come to get shot yesterday?' Hatfield asked.

''Cordin' to his story, he was ridin' the Mescalero about two miles east of the Runnin' W ranchhouse, aimin' to cut south-west at the forks to his place, when a jigger throwed lead at him outa the dark. He figgered by the shots that there were several of the hellions holed up in the brush, so he cut and run for it, circled and made it to his spread. Wasn't much to the wound—just a shallow furrow in his arm above the elbow—so he patched it up and waited until morning to ride in and have me dress it. I put the arm in a sling to ease it. He'll have the use of it in a week.'

'Shot at east of the Running W ranchhouse,' Hatfield mused. 'What time did it happen?'

'Coupla hours before midnight, I believe he said,' Doc replied.

'And just about that time I was shot west of the ranchhouse,' Hatfield reflected. 'Looks like those hellions post men on each side of where they figger to pull something—to guard against interruption.'

'Could be, admittin' that Wyman told the truth about what happened,' Doc agreed.

'Yuh're not sure he told the truth?'

Doctor Beard countered with a question of his own.

'Yuh say somebody throwed lead at you last night? Which means, seein' as yuh're still kickin', that yuh did in or winged one or more of 'em? That right?'

'Well, there was a mite of yelling after I pulled trigger,' Hatfield admitted. 'But the hellions managed to hightail through the brush.'

'Hmmm!' commented Doc. 'Well, I'm not expressin' any opinion, but I'm passin' on to you what folks say. Among other things, they say the hellion who appears to give the orders to the Death Riders is a big tall jigger and rides a black horse, a mighty fine one. Did yuh happen to notice what Wyman was forkin' when he left the hitchrack across the street?'

'Plenty of honest folks ride black horses,' Hatfield protested.

'Uh-huh, and I'm not sayin' anythin' against Wyman. I'm just passin' on the talk to you. But just the same, the Death Rider business shore picked up a couple months back, right after Wyman stopped makin' hair bridles.'

Hatfield stood up, towering over the old doctor, who was himself a lanky six-footer.

'Wyman and Burns Wright didn't get along, then?' he remarked.

'Nope, they didn't. Wyman was sorta friendly with old Cale Wright, who owned the Runnin' W; after Burns come over from Arizona where, I understand, he owned a small spread hc sold out at a good profit, and took the job as foreman under old Cale, Wyman stopped droppin' in at the Runnin' W like he usta. Some fellers just nacherly don't get along, and I reckon that was the case with Wyman and Burns Wright.'

Hatfield nodded thoughtfully. 'Well, be seein' yuh soon, Doc,' he said, and departed to hunt up Stiffy Jones.

Hatfield had no trouble locating the Dust Layer saloon which was housed in a two-story false-front a few doors below Doc Beard's office. Light gleamed behind the broad plate-glass window and a babble of talk came over the swinging doors.

Although it was little past mid-afternoon, Hatfield found the big room pretty well crowded when he entered. The long, mirror-blazing bar was lined, there were several poker games in progress at tables and two roulette wheels and a faro bank were doing business. A sizeable dance floor was vacant as yet and the chairs of the orchestra, which occupied a small raised platform, were unoccupied. A lunch counter spanning a section of the far end of the room had a sprinkling of customers. Others ate in more leisurely fashion at tables reserved for their use.

There was a mixed company in the Dust Layer. Hatfield catalogued the majority of the customers as cowhands, but there were men wearing laced boots and corduroys. Miners from the hills to the north, he deduced, or perhaps workers from the railroad construction camps south-west of the town. There were also men in riding garb who did not fit into either category. Although their costume was practically identical with that of the cowhands, there was a subtle difference about them that set them apart from the workers of neighbourhood spreads. Some might be chuckline riding cowboys, Hatfield decided. Others belonged to the brand of gentry with doubtful antecedents, questionable presents and doubtful futures, the Lone Wolf shrewdly suspected. The kind that always, sooner or later, show up in a section undergoing a boom.

Swift glances were darted in his direction as Hatfield entered. He knew he was being covertly studied by more than one pair of eyes present, doubtless the reception accorded any stranger.

At the far end of the bar he saw Stiffy Jones conversing with a tall, well set up, straight-featured man with hard eyes and a tight mouth.

Stiffy, already half drunk, greeted the Ranger boisterously.

'Come on and have a drink,' he invited. 'Hatfield, I want yuh to know Wade Hansford. Wade owns these diggin's.'

Hansford shook hands with a firm grip. Hatfield noted that his watchful eyes were so darkly blue as to seem black under certain lights. He had an affable manner and a smile that somewhat relieved the hard set of his thin-lipped mouth.

'Stiffy was just telling me what yuh did over to the Running W ranchhouse,' he remarked. 'It was a mighty fine thing to do.'

'Didn't get any results,' Hatfield deprecated.

'Even so, that didn't lessen the courage of the act,' Hansford replied. 'It wasn't yore fault there was nobody there to rescue. Not many men would take a chance like that, and it denoted mighty fast thinking, too. Yuh say yuh found pore Burns Wright's bones in the ashes?'

'Yes, we found bones,' Hatfield admitted.

'And there weren't nobody but Burns in the house when the fire started,' Stiffy said. 'They were his bones, all right.'

'Burns usta drop in here quite frequent,' remarked Hansford. 'He played a good hand of poker and was mighty nifty at handling cards. He woulda made a good dealer. I told him so, more'n once. Even offered him a job once. Could use him to-day,' he added with a laugh. 'Last night my best man didn't show up. Hasn't showed up to-day, either.'

'That would be Pete Spencer, wouldn't it?' put in Stiffy. 'What become of him?'

Hansford shrugged his broad shoulders.

'Hell only knows,' he replied. 'Yuh never can tell about dealers, or gamblers of any sort, for that matter. They're here to-day and gone to-morrow. Mebbe somebody who knew him dropped into town and Pete decided some other climate might be healthier. I run straight games here, but it isn't so in all places. Mebbe Pete dealt at a place where they weren't over particklar as to which end of a deck the cards came from. Might have got caught cold decking or with a clip in his sleeve. Dealers trail their twine sudden after that, if they're able to trail it, and when the past catches up with them they usually trail again. I've a notion Pete caught a train or the stage outa here in a hurry. I don't expect to see him again, but I got a coupla swampers looking around town for him on the chance he's drunk and asleep under a table.'

Hatfield nodded his understanding and they had another drink together. They were discussing it with appreciation when the swinging doors banged open and a little old man scudded through as if blown by the wind, his grey whiskers fanning out on either side of his ashen face, his hair positively bristling on his head. He glared about, spotted Hansford and streaked across the room.

'I found him!' he screeched. 'He's behind the door!'

Hansford regarded him disgustedly.

'Yuh sure got a load on in a hurry, Anse,' he grunted. 'Who's behind the door—a boa constrictor, or is it a pink elephant with a blue tail?'

'Pete Spencer!' squalled the old swamper. 'The door shoved hard, and when I looked behind it there he was, with a knife in his back!'

## CHAPTER THREE

## THE WIDELOOPERS STRIKE

It took a good shake on the part of Hansford and a brimming glass of whisky to render the old fellow coherent.

'I'd done looked everywhere,' he finally explained. 'Decided it might be a good bet to look in his room.'

'That's the last place anybody ever looks when one of those pasteboard shufflers show up missing,' interpolated Hansford. 'Go on, Anse.'

'The door was locked and nobody answered when I pounded on it,' explained Anse. 'I hunted up the landlord and he got a key and opened the door. We hadda shove like hell to get it open, and when we looked to see what was makin' it stick, there was pore Pete deader'n a bottle of beer what's stood open all night. He was layin' on his face, and there was blood on the floor and the handle of a big knife stickin' outa his back. I come away from there, pronto.'

'Yuh look like yuh did,' admitted Hansford. 'Did yuh stop at the sheriff's office?'

'Didn't stop nowhere,' grunted Anse. 'I was goin' so fast that I skidded four doors past here before I could get stopped.'

'Looks like somebody who usta know Pete *did* drop into town,' Hansford remarked. 'Come on, Anse, let's go to his room and look things over. You fellers like to come along?'

Hatfield and Stiffy Jones agreed that they would. Hansford called the head bartender and gave him instructions, then they hurried out together. At the door, Hansford turned to the swamper.

'You hustle up to the sheriff's office and notify the deputy,' he directed. 'Tell him we'll be in Pete's room.'

Pete Spencer was not a pretty object. His shirt was crusted with dry blood and his limbs were contorted. On his dead face was frozen a peculiar expression.

'Looks like he was more surprised than scairt,' muttered Hansford.

Hatfield also thought that the expression on the dead man's face was one of utter astonishment and unbelief. His black brows drew together as he regarded the rigid features.

'Almost like he was done in by somebody he knew well and had no reason to fear,' Hatfield said.

Hansford nodded. 'Sure dead, all right,' he remarked. 'Well, this leaves me short a dealer the day before payday at the mines and the railroad construction camp. Hell! Ever deal cards, Hatfield?'

'Afraid my hand isn't in good enough shape to handle a table in a place like yores,' Hatfield smiled. 'How about Stiffy?'

'That old hellion couldn't get his hand into a barrel without bustin' a stave,' growled Hansford. 'All he's good for is to deal 'em off the bar to his mouth.'

'That's a lie,' declared the injured Stiffy. 'I eat, too.'

'Not if yuh have a chance to drink instead,' said Hansford. 'Here comes the deputy.'

Trout Mason clumped into the room and glanced about. Old Anse trailed nervously behind him.

'See business is keepin' up,' he commented. 'Who did him in, Wade?'

'Hell knows,' replied Hansford. 'Anse found him a little while ago. 'Pears to have been dead for twenty-four hours, at least. He didn't show up for work last night. Reckon it happened before that.'

'We'll have that damn town so cluttered up with bodies somebody'll have to move out to make room,' growled the deputy. 'I'm expectin' Mack Bush in any minute with a couple more—them two Runnin' W hands who were did in up at Skeleton Canyon, and I understand there's three more out at the Runnin' W ranchhouse. Wonder who's next?'

'Yuh needn't be lookin' at me,' said Stiffy Jones. 'Pick on Anse there—he's lived too long, anyhow.'

'I'm younger'n you, yuh dadgummed stoved-up pelican,' bawled the insulted swamper. 'You'd be dead right now if yuh wasn't pickled in alcohol.'

'I figger they'll hafta kill both of yuh with a club to get the Resurrection Day started,' grunted Hansford.

Jim Hatfield asked a question:

'Yuh say the door was locked when yuh tried

to get in, Anse?'

'That's right,' agreed the swamper.

'S'pose yuh give the body a once-over, Deputy,' Hatfield suggested.

'Might be a good idea,' nodded Mason. He proceeded to go through the dead man's pockets, unearthing a miscellany of articles and considerable money.

'Robbery wasn't the motive, anyhow,' he remarked. A moment later he drew forth a bunch of keys.

'And it looks like the killer didn't leave by way of the door,' Hatfield remarked, 'and I've a notion he didn't come in that way, either,' he added, walking to the open window across the room.

'Thought so,' he nodded. 'See that tree growing outside the window, Deputy, and that big branch stretching alongside the window-sill and not three feet from it? Look how the bark is scuffed on the top of the branch. Reckon the knife-handling gent slid in by way of that, mebbe slipped up on Spencer or waited until he came in. And I've a notion Spencer got a good look at him before he used the knife.'

'How yuh figger that?' demanded the deputy.

'Take a good look at Spencer's face,' Hatfield suggested. 'Wouldn't yuh say from the expression froze on it that he'd just had a big surprise? So big, in fact, that it left its mark even after death.'

'It does look that way,' admitted Mason, 'and I believe yuh're right about that branch, too. Say, yuh don't miss much, do yuh? Yuh'd make a good detective, or a deputy sheriff.'

'Take the job of dealing I offered yuh fust, Hatfield,' said Wade Hansford. 'It'll give yuh a higher standing in the community. Dealers hafta be intelligent.'

'That's right,' agreed Mason. 'They make saloon-keepers outa the dumb ones.'

Hansford grinned. 'I'll hafta be getting back to my place,' he said. 'Can't leave it too long, with all those smart dealers around.'

'I'll go tell Doc Beard about this,' said Mason. 'Doc'll be so busy holdin' inquests he won't have time to pizen anybody for the next week.'

The sheriff and his posse got in shortly after nightfall. He didn't bring any rustlers with him, but he did bring two blanket-draped forms, the remains of the two Running W cowhands who had been downed by the wideloopers.

The rest of the Running W outfit accompanied the sheriff to town. Their reception of old Stiffy's story was luridly profane, and after receiving the news of the outrage at the Running W ranchhouse, they repaired to the Dust Layer and proceeded to drown their sorrows.

Old Stiffy's story had lost nothing in the telling and they gave Hatfield a boisterous welcome to their midst. They proved to be a likeable bunch of reckless, carefree young fellows.

'We're just gettin' to know each other well,' one confided to the Lone Wolf. 'Ain't been together but a month or so. Burns Wright got us together from spreads over east of here. Dropped into towns over there offerin' good wages. Seems he had a bad row with his old hands a spell back and they all quit on him except Stiffy and pore old Billy and Hank. They were too old to go sashayin' around, I reckon, so they stayed on. Wright was a good man to work for, only he wouldn't stand for no foolishness and he had his own notions about runnin' spread. Reckon them notions didn't allus set over well with the old hands who had worked for his brother a long time before he died. Can't say as I agree with everythin' he does, so far as that goes. For instance, I can't see a owner practically strippin' a spread like he did with the Runnin' W to get that herd together. Of co'hse he got a good price for the beefs, but he didn't leave much for breeders. Mebbe he was figgerin' on stockin' up with some other kind of breeds, though hell knows where he woulda got 'em from. Reckon that big herd is south of the Rio Grande by now.'

'Yuh hadn't delivered the herd to the Circle J when it was widelooped?'

'That's right,' the puncher agreed.

'Then the sale wasn't really consummated, even though Wright had received payment?'

'Reckon that's right, too. Burns rode on ahead and collected the pay from Buster, I understand. Said he wanted to get to town to the bank with it before dark. The Wrights and the Busters were neighbours for years, I heard, and I reckon Buster figgered it would be all right. He'd already looked over the herd and was satisfied with his bargain.'

'I see. But under the circumstances, it looks like the Running W not only lost the herd, but will hafta make good the money Buster put out, seeing it was lost while in Wright's hands. Stiffy said he saw Wright put the money into the safe at the ranchhouse. He didn't ride to the bank after all.'

'Reckon he musta been held up and figgered he couldn't get there before closin' time,' the cowboy hazarded.

'Looks that way,' Hatfield agreed.

'The spread is sure gonna be hard hit,' the puncher muttered. 'Don't know how it will affect us fellers. We may be out of a job. I've a notion the boys won't care over much, though. I understand the new owner is a woman—due to land here to-morrow—and fellers like us don't take over well to workin' for a lady boss.'

'Most hands don't,' Hatfield admitted. His eyes were thoughtful as he raised his glass and sipped from it. He left the Dust Layer a little later and visited Doc Beard.

'I'll sit to-morrow mornin' on that dealer and the bodies of them punchers Mack Bush brought in,' Doc said. 'But I figger to wait until Miss Teri gets here before holdin' an inquest at the ranch. I understand she's due to-morrow on the noon train. I wish you'd ride out to the spread to-morrow mornin' and see to it everythin' is under control, Hatfield. Have Stiffy and the boys sorta tidy things up a mite. It's gonna be hard on that gal at the best. She's young—not more'n twenty-one. She was just a few months past twenty when she went back to college last fall. Fust her father is done in, and now her uncle. Yeah, it's gonna be hard on her.'

'She's coming home to plenty of trouble, from what I hear, Doc,' Hatfield remarked. 'According to what those Running W hands told me a little while ago, the spread is pretty well stripped of cows and she'll hafta make good that twenty thousand dollars to Buster as well. She's liable to have trouble holding on to the ranch.'

'Buster won't push her any more'n he has to,' Doc replied with confidence. 'He's a good old injun, but I've a notion he ain't in any position to lose twenty thousand dollars right now. He's like so many cowmen—he's land poor. Got good acres, but nothin' much else. He's been figgerin' on gettin' ahead with his sales to the railroad construction camp. But he won't push her any more'n he has to. Him and Cale Wright were neighbours and good friends for a lot of years, I understand.'

Hatfield said good night to the doctor and went to bed in the room he had rented near where Goldy, his big sorrel, was stabled. He was up early the next morning and after breakfast at the Dust Layer, which served excellent food in addition to whisky no worse than the average, he saddled up and headed for the Running W. Old Stiffy, he ascertained, had gone back to the spread the night before, little the worse for the redeye he had consumed.

Hatfield rode at a leisurely pace, letting Goldy take his time up the steep grade from the town to where the trail leveled off as it followed the slope of the range of hills. He wanted time to think and did not push the sorrel, even after the crest of the sag was reached. Above him the hill tops loomed against the blue Texas sky, with a long slope swelling upward to their rounded crests.

Below the trail the slope continued, dropping sharply downward to the floor of the desert, perhaps five hundred yards lower down. At the base of the slope, Hatfield could see a gleam of steel where the twin ribbons of the railroad vanished east and west around shoulders of the hills.

Hatfield had covered perhaps two-thirds of the distance to the Running W ranchhouse when he noted, at the base of the steep, boulder-strewn, brush-grown slope, a long trestle spanning a deep and wide dry wash. At the far end of this trestle a group of men were busying themselves over something.

'Railroad section hands making repairs on the trestle or the track,' the Lone Wolf surmised, idly watching their activities as he rode. At the same moment he mechanically noted a low mutter that was vibrating the air and steadily growing louder.

'Train coming,' he told his horse. 'Sounds like a fast passenger.'

He was directly above the west end of the trestle and the industrious workmen at the time. He watched them curiously, wondering indifferently why a flagman was not out to whistle notification that the train was drawing near as was customary under such circumstances.

Suddenly the group turned and headed away from the track at a fast pace. Hatfield abruptly stiffened. He leaned forward in his saddle, peering intently at the men below. The bright sunlight struck full upon them revealing black faces streaked with white. Seen at closer range, those streaks would doubtless form the pattern of a skull on the black background!

Without an instant's hesitation, Jim Hatfield sent Goldy over the lip of the trail and skittering downward over the loose boulders and through the tall brush that littered the lower slope.

## Chapter Four

# A MAN AND A MAID

The C & P Flyer, eastbound, was late and making up time. In the cab of the roaring locomotive the old engineer bounced about on his seatbox, glanced at his water glass and steam gauge, gazed keenly at the track ahead. A hot glare filled the cab as the fireman swung open the firebox door. The musical clang of a shovel on the steel apron sounded as he bailed black diamonds into the raging furnace. He closed the door, hopped on to his own seatbox and glanced complacently at the feathery squirrel-tail of steam that curled back from the safety-valve, a guarantee that the steam gauge needle was wavering against the two-hundred-pound pressure mark. Behind the labouring locomotive the long string of yellow coaches rolled smoothly along, swaying on the curves, dazzling beams of sunlight reflecting back from their glistening windows. The locomotive drive wheels ground the high iron, the siderods clanked a flickering blur. The air was redolent with the smell of coal smoke and hot oil.

Around a curve lurched the flying engine. The engineer stared steadily ahead to where a trestle spanned a wide dry wash.

'Say,' he exclaimed suddenly, as his peering eyes noted a swirl of blue smoke trickling up from the end of the trestle, 'looks like there's a fire over there. Can't be much to it, though, from the looks of the smoke, but we'd better report it when we get to Creston. It—God A'mighty!'

From the end of the trestle had mushroomed a cloud of yellow smoke. Hurtling through the tumbling masses were crossties, splintered beams and twisted rails. A crackling explosion sounded above the pound of steel on steel.

The engineer slammed the throttle shut, twisted his airbrake handle frantically and 'wiped the gauge'. Air screamed through the port, the brake shoes ground against the wheels, shooting out showers of sparks that glittered palely golden in the sunlight. Brake rigging clanged along the length of the coaches. There was a prodigious banging of couplers. The locomotive bucked, leaped like a living thing, slowed almost instantly, then surged ahead under the pile-driver slam of the following coaches.

Madly the old hogger fought to save his train. Over came the reverse bar, he jerked the throttle wide open, twirled the sand blowers to send streams of sand spouting beneath the tires of the great drive wheels that were spinning in reverse. But again came that mighty surge of the flying coaches. The engine shot ahead, tortured wheels shrieking protest.

'I can't hold 'em!' yelled the engineer. 'Leave her!'

The white-faced fireman was already crouched on the lowest cab step. He took a deep breath and leaped far out from the rocketing engine. He hit the ground hard, bounced high into the air, came down a-sprawl, rolled over and over and lay still and senseless on the desert sand. Past him howled the locomotive with bellowing stack and grinding drivers.

The engineer waited until the last possible moment. With the pilot of the locomotive reaching for the yawning chasm that had been the end of the trestle, he hurled himself through the cab window. He also struck hard, but managed to stagger to his feet, blood running down his face.

With a stupendous crash, the locomotive plunged to the bottom of the wash, a crash followed almost instantly by the thundering roar of the exploding boiler.

The express car behind the engine, its windows smashed to splinters, its sliding doors wrenched wide open and jammed in their slots by the terrific impact, teetered precariously with a third of its length hanging over the gulf. The coaches were a-bellow with the yells and screams of the bruised and terrified passengers.

From the brush that flanked the right-of-way streamed masked features, the white streakings on their black masks resolving to crudely done death's heads. Guns in hands, they rushed towards the express car.

There was a crack of a gun from the darkened interior of the car. One of the wreckers howled a curse and pawed at his face down which blood was streaming from under his mask. Again the unseen gun cracked and a second raider staggered as a bullet clipped his arm.

With yells and curses, the owlhoots turned and fled back to the cover of the growth. For several moments nothing broke the silence save the continued cries of the passengers struggling with the jammed coach doors.

Something sailed from the brush leaving a trail of bluish smoke streaming after it. The hurtling object vanished through the door of the express car. Almost instantly there was a booming explosion. Smoke gushed from the door of the car, whirling and eddying in the clear air. As it cleared, the car stood shadowy and silent, void of life or motion.

Again the bandits emerged from cover. No shots greeted them. They hesitated, staring at the car, darting keen glances along the length of the coaches.

'That did for the blankety-blanks,' a tall man in front of the others shouted harshly. 'Welch, you and Jasper watch them coaches. Don't let anybody come out. Come along, the rest of yuh.'

He led the rush to the shadowy door of the silent express car. Gripping the ledge with both hands, he started to lower his body through the opening. He jerked his head around at a sudden crashing in the brush at the base of the slope, gave a yelp of consternation.

From the straggle of growth burst a great golden horse, eyes rolling, nostrils flaring red, his glorious black mane tossing in the wind. His rider, crouched low in the saddle, eyes glinting in the shadow of his hatbrim, held a long black gun in each hand. Instantly those black gun muzzles streamed fire and smoke. The air rocked to the echo of the thunderous reports.

Under the blast of those thundering guns the train wreckers scattered in wild confusion. One gave a queer strangled cough and pitched forward on his face. A second spun round and round like a top released from the string and went down kicking and clawing on the sand. The others fired wildly in reply, but the golden horse was doing a weird, elusive dance that made him as easy to shoot at as a sunbeam glinting on the crest of a wave.

His erratic movements apparently did not affect the aim of his tall rider. A third bandit gave a howl of pain and rage and pawed madly at a blood-spouting arm. The shock of the heavy slug almost bowled him over, but he kept his feet, ducked his head and dived into the bushes like a scared rabbit.

His retreat was the signal for universal panic. Yelling and cursing, the other outlaws scudded after him to vanish among the growth.

Instantly the rider of the golden horse slid his smoking sixes into their sheaths and jerked a heavy Winchester from the saddle boot snugged under his left thigh. He flung the long gun to his shoulder and sent a stream of lead hissing and crackling into the bushes. The ejection lever of his rifle worked so fast it was but a filmy blur of gleaming metal in the sunlight. Echoing the reports came a wild crashing and the staccato click of horses' irons on the stones.

The rifleman leaped from the back of his weaving horse and, bending almost double, raced into the growth. Silently as a prowling wolf, and as swiftly, he wormed his way through the brush, taking advantage of every bit of cover, his green eyes probing the bushes ahead, every muscle tense for instant action. Behind the final fringe that flanked a little clearing shouldering against the base of the slope he paused, listening and peering. From the distance ahead came the rattle of hoofs, fast diminishing in volume.

Jim Hatfield listened a moment longer, automatically filling the magazine of his rifle with fresh cartridges. Hooking it under his arm, he reloaded his empty Colts. Then, satisfied that the Death Riders had had a bellyful and were sifting sand away from there, he retraced his steps to the pandemonium of the wrecked train.

The passengers had gotten the jammed doors open and were streaming from the coaches, shouting and gesticulating. A wild babble of questions arose.

A scared and bloody face protruded cautiously around the door jamb of the express car.

'Anybody bad hurt in there?' Hatfield called.

'My pardner's knocked out, but he ain't dead,' the messenger replied. 'Gosh! cowboy, but yuh come in a good time! I figgered we were all goners.'

The passengers were crowding around the wrecked express car, talking and gesturing excitedly. The blue-uniformed conductor hurried up.

'Nobody bad hurt,' he said. 'The engineer is skinned up a bit and the fireman had all the breath knocked outa him for a minute, but he come around all right. No passengers wuss than bruised or scratched. How is it up here?'

'My pardner's comin' outa it,' the messenger called from inside the car. His bruised face appeared again.

'And they didn't get the mines' payroll, either, thanks to this big feller,' he exulted. 'Blazes! I never seed such shootin'! He downed two of 'em and knocked dust outa a couple more. Reckon this is one time them blankety-blank Death Riders bit off more'n they could chaw!'

Hatfield strode to the two dead raiders and

jerked the paint-streaked masks from their faces, revealing hard-bitten countenances contorted in the agony of death.

'Anybody recognize them?' he asked of the group crowding around him.

There was a universal shaking of heads.

'Mean lookin' cusses,' grunted the conductor. 'That one on the right looks like he might have Injun blood.'

Hatfield began emptying the pockets of the unsavoury pair.

'Might be something to tie them up with some outfit or other,' he explained.

But there was nothing identifying in the odds and ends the pockets revealed, nor anything unusual until Hatfield drew from one a small silver rod about eight inches long with a smooth round ball forming one end.

'That's a funny lookin' ditty,' remarked the conductor, who was bending over watching the search. 'Wonder what the hell it is?'

Hatfield did not reply directly, although the concentration furrow deepened between his black brows as he fingered the tapering bit of metal with the ball at the larger end.

'Think I'll keep this as a souvenir,' he remarked casually, slipping it into his pocket.

'Reckon yuh earned it,' the conductor remarked cheerfully. 'I usta know a jigger, a *muy male hombre*, who cut off an ear from every gent he cashed in. Had quite a collection—smoked 'em, and lined 'em up on the mantelpiece of his cabin. Usually carried the latest one in his vest pocket for a spell.'

'Haven't got a mantelpiece,' Hatfield grinned, 'but it's a notion, all right.'

The paint on the masks worn by the wreckers seemed to interest the Lone Wolf. He scratched at it with a tentative fingernail, cupped his hands around one of the streaks and gazed at it long and earnestly, his black brows drawing together in thought. Finally he folded the squares of black silk and put them in his pockets.

'More souvenirs,' he told the conductor. 'Besides, the sheriff will want to see them, and they might get lost if I left them here.'

The dead bandits wore ordinary range costumes, much the same as Hatfield's, consisting of faded blue shirts, overalls, batwing chaps and high-heeled boots of softly tanned leather. Each carried a heavy gun sagging from a well-filled cartridge belt. Their battered 'J.B.' lay on the sand nearby. Hatfield looked at the sweat bands of the wide-brimmed hats for possible names or initials, but found none. He straightened up, glancing around him.

'Look out!' a passenger yelled. 'Here's one comin' back!'

Hatfield turned quickly, slim hands dropping to his gun butts. Riding from the brush into which the bandits had vanished was a tall young man forking a fine black horse. His left arm was suspended across his breast by a sling. Hatfield recognized Tom Wyman, the young ranch owner who had had trouble with the law the year before.

Wyman pulled up a few paces distant, speculating on the scene with curious eyes. He dismounted somewhat clumsily because of his injured arm and strode forward. Abruptly he halted and stood staring, apparently forgetful of everything except the slender girl with wide blue eyes and honey-coloured hair upon whom his intent gaze was focused.

Hatfield had already noticed the girl among the milling passengers. At variance with the costumes of her fellow travellers, she was garbed in a riding habit that showed signs of considerable use. As her glance met Wyman's, one sun-golden little hand flew to her lips. The colour drained from her face, then returned in a rush that dyed her cheeks scarlet.

'*Tom!*' Hatfield heard her breathe in a voice that quavered with emotion.

Apparently oblivious of the crowd, Wyman took a step towards her.

'Teri!' he said. 'I heard yuh were comin' back today! And yuh were on this train! God!'

Abruptly the girl seemed to remember that many eyes were upon her. She smiled brightly, and extended her hand.

'How are you, Tom?' she asked in easy conversational tones. 'I'm glad to see you, even under such unusual circumstances.'

'Yuh're all right? Not hurt?' Wyman asked in anxious tones.

'Perfectly all right and not hurt a bit, just scared half out of my wits. How is everything at the Running W? And how is Uncle Burns?'

Wyman started. His face was suddenly drawn. He took her by the arm and gently led her out of earshot.

The other passengers and the train crew, seeing nothing unusual in evident old acquaintances meeting and having something to talk about, resumed their discussion of the recent stirring happenings. Hatfield, however, watched the pair intently. He saw the girl's breath catch as Wyman spoke earnestly in low tones, and her face again whiten. Her voice suddenly rose and her words were audible to his keen ears.

'I must get to the spread at once,' she said. She glanced helplessly at the smashed trestle. 'And the train won't be able to get across for hours, maybe days!'

'Yuh can have my horse, Teri, he can make it up the slope,' Wyman replied. 'Only—'

He glanced anxiously about. 'Those hellions are liable to be most anywhere,' Hatfield heard him say. 'If my cayuse would only carry double—but he won't.'

'I'm not afraid,' the girl said.

But Wyman still looked worried and hesitant.

Jim Hatfield walked over to the pair.

'Excuse me, Ma'am,' he said in his deep, musical voice, 'but I couldn't help hearing this gent speak yore name. Yuh're Miss Teri Wright, aren't yuh?'

'That's right,' the girl replied wonderingly. 'How do you know—'

'Why yuh're the feller who was goin' inter Doc Beard's office with old Stiffy Jones when I came out, aren't yuh?' Wyman broke in. 'I heard about yuh. Yore name's Hatfield, isn't it?'

Hatfield nodded smilingly, and held out his hand.

'Tom Wyman, isn't it? Doc Beard was speaking of yuh yesterday. Glad to have a chance to know yuh, Wyman.'

Wyman stared, seemed to hesitate, then took Hatfield's hand in a firm grip.

'I was just going to say,' the Lone Wolf remarked, 'that I was on my way to the Running W when I got mixed up in this little shindig. If Miss Wright is agreeable, I'll ride with her, seeing that she's nacherly anxious to get there in a hurry and yuh don't like the notion of her riding alone, Wyman.'

'That will be fine,' the young rancher replied gratefully and without an instant's hesitation. 'I'll feel a heap sight easier in my mind if you do that, Hatfield.'

'Come to see me soon, Tom,' the girl urged.

Wyman seemed to hesitate. He flushed darkly.

'I don't know, Teri,' he said. 'Yuh know—folks will talk.'

The girl was about to reply when Hatfield spoke.

'Wyman,' he said, 'I figger the way things are at her spread, the little lady is going to need a good, trustworthy man to give her a hand. I reckon yuh better be on the job.'

Suddenly he smiled down at the pair, a flashing wide smile that made his stern face wonderfully pleasant.

'Walk yore road, son,' he said softly. 'It may seem a rough road at times, but there's no road so rough a *man* can't walk it, and usually he's the better for the tough going if he *is* a man.'

Young Tom Wyman stared at the tall Ranger to whom, although he was a stalwart six-footer himself, he was forced to lift his glance considerably. He drew a deep breath, squared his broad shoulders.

'Okay,' he said, 'I'll be seein' yuh soon, Teri. I'm headin' for my spread, now. It's only a coupla miles to the south-west of here,' he added for Hatfield's benefit.

'Just a minute,' Hatfield told the girl. He walked over to the conductor.

'How about yore train and passengers?' he asked.

'There'll be a wreck train out here from Creston mighty soon when we don't show up on time,' the conductor replied. 'They'll know somethin' has happened.'

'Okay,' Hatfield nodded. 'Better get yore passengers back in the coaches and tell these express messengers to keep their eyes open and their guns handy. I don't figger those hellions will come back, but it doesn't pay to take chances with an outfit like that.'

'They'll get a hot reception if they do,' the conductor promised grimly.

Hatfield returned to the girl.

'We'll tackle that slope now if yuh're ready, Ma'am,' he said.

The slope was a hard chore even for Goldy, and Wyman's big black was taxed to his uttermost, but they finally made it to the trail without mishap.

'Tell me,' the girl exclaimed suddenly as they rode westward, 'do you always have the effect on people that you had on Tom Wyman? Tom looked as if a big load had been lifted from his shoulders after you spoke to him.'

'I reckon most any feller needs a word at times to help him over a rough spot,' Hatfield equivocated.

'Poor Tom,' she said, speaking in that soft, caressing voice which Jim Hatfield had long noted only the best of women possess, 'I'm afraid he is terribly embittered by—by what happened to him.

'We—we were going to be married,' she added, 'and—and then—'

'Don't see any sense in putting it off any

longer,' Hatfield said cheerfully. 'The Bible says it isn't good for a man to live alone, and I reckon that goes double for a woman.'

'That's the way I feel about it,' Teri admitted, colouring prettily. 'But Tom is terribly proud, and he feels deeply about what happened. I wrote to him while he was—away, but he never answered.'

She turned her blue eyes to the Ranger, her flower-like little face uplifted, and Hatfield saw there was a misting of tears on her long, dark lashes.

'Tell me,' she said, 'do you believe he was guilty of—of what they charged him with?'

'No,' Hatfield replied quietly, 'I don't.'

The girl gave a long, quivering sigh.

'I feel a lot better,' she said. 'Not because I have any doubts that need resolving, but because it's so good to know somebody else believes in him.'

Soon afterward they reached the site of the Running W ranchhouse. Old Stiffy Jones gave them a boisterous greeting. The Running W hands standing about, hat in hand, were awkward and diffident at first but Teri Wright soon put them at their ease. A little while after she had talked with each in turn Jim Hatfield strolled over to the young puncher with whom he had spoken in the Dust Layer the night before.

'Still figger yuh don't care to work for a lady boss?' he asked, his voice solemn, but with a merry light in the depths of his strangely coloured eyes.

'Say, feller!' the cowboy exclaimed enthusiastically, 'I'd work for her without pay!'

Hatfield chuckled, and walked away, well satisfied in his mind.

Soon afterward, Doc Beard, the sheriff and the coroner's jury arrived, talking excitedly about the wreck they had observed from the trail.

The sheriff was a grumpy old-timer with a querulous expression. Doc Beard beckoned to Hatfield and introduced him. Hatfield drew Doc and the sheriff aside and in a few terse sentences related what had happened at the trestle at the base of the slope. Doc clucked indignantly. The sheriff swore luridly and shook his fist at the sky.

The coroner's jury's verdict on the bodies of the two old cowboys and the blanket of charred bones was short and laconic, and typical of the cow country:

Burns Wright, Hank Masters and Billy Summervill (it read) came to their death at the hands of parties unknown who have a hanging coming. We recommend the sheriff brings in the Death Riders pronto.

* * *

Sheriff Bush let out an indignant yelp when the verdict was read.

'Bring 'em in!' he bawled. 'Bring 'em in, hell! I can't even get within shootin' distance of the blankety-blanks!'

'Easy, Mack,' cautioned old Doc, 'there's a lady within hearin' distance.'

Sheriff Bush subsided to incoherent sputterings. Doc chuckled, and went to confer with Jim Hatfield.

Later, Hatfield had another conference, with Teri Wright in the Running W bunkhouse. The yellow-haired girl came to the point with the brevity and directness of the rangeland.

'I badly need a foreman to take charge of the spread,' she told the Lone Wolf. 'Will you take the job? I don't know as yet in what shape the finances of the outfit are, but I will be able to pay the hands for a while, anyhow. I have some money, not a great deal, left me by my grandmother, apart from the ranch. I intend to put that into the operation of the spread.'

Hatfield considered a moment, gazing thoughtfully out the window at the charred ribs of the burned ranchhouse. He needed an excuse for hanging around the section and he had a feeling that the Running W was going to be the focal point of activity.

'Okay, Ma'am,' he said at length, 'yuh've hired yoreself a hand.'

Teri herself made the announcement to the cowboys; it was received enthusiastically. Hatfield immediately issued his first orders.

'Right off, we've got to put up a temporary place for Miss Teri to live in,' he told them. 'We'll go about building a regular *casa* as we have the time to spare. Before that, though, I've a notion there is another more important chore to attend to.'

Two days later, after the funerals of the dead hands and the pathetic bundle of charred bones, Hatfield's hunch proved correct. He and Teri Wright rode to town where the girl talked with the bank officials and old Banks Buster, owner of the Circle J.

'The spread is broke,' the girl told him as they sat over a meal in the Dust Layer. 'Broke and in debt. Mr Buster has agreed to receive the twenty thousand dollars lost in the robbery in instalments. I gave him a note for twenty thousand dollars with the spread as security. So long as I can meet the payments, he won't foreclose. He is willing to help me all he can, but he is hard pressed for money himself. He was very generous and nullified the contract my uncle made with him to supply him with regular cattle shipments which he needs to fill his own contract with the railroad construction camp.'

Hatfield glanced up quickly.

'Nullified it, did he?'

'That's right,' the girl replied.

'That's good news,' Hatfield told her.

'Why?' she asked wonderingly.

'Because,' Hatfield said, 'now yuh can sell

direct to the railroad and make a larger profit.'

'But I doubt if they will buy from me,' she replied. 'As I understand it, they will deal only with large shippers.'

Jim Hatfield smiled slightly.

'I've a notion they'll deal with you,' he told her. 'I sorta know a feller who works for the road and I've a notion he'll agree to lend yuh a hand.'

'I wonder if I have any cattle to sell?' Teri remarked. 'Stiffy Jones says they very nearly stripped the spread to get that last herd together.'

'I never yet saw a spread where yuh couldn't root out a hefty passel of fat beefs from the brakes and canyons, if yuh really go after them,' Hatfield said. 'I've a notion yuh'll find that's the condition here. We'll make a try at it.'

He smoked thoughtfully for several minutes over a final cup of steaming coffee, then adroitly turned the conversation into another channel.

'Yore uncle was a good cattleman?' he asked.

'I think so,' the girl replied. 'I never knew much about him. You see, he wasn't really my uncle. His name wasn't even Wright, though most people have forgotten about that.'

'Wasn't yore uncle?'

'No, only a step-uncle. He was not my

father's brother. My grandfather Wright married a second time, late in life. The widow lady he married had a young son, and that son became the man known as Burns Wright—he took my grandfather's name. His real name was Burns Colver. He and my father never got along very well. I don't think Dad was overly pleased when he came back from Arizona last year. It was lucky for me, however, as I had someone to leave in charge of the spread while I was finishing college. Poor Uncle Burns! It would have been better for him to have stayed in Arizona the way things worked out.'

'Yes,' Hatfield agreed, 'I've a notion it would. Yuh say he had been in Arizona?'

'Yes, for several years. I don't know just where. If I had, the chances are I would have stopped off in Arizona to visit with him during one of my trips to school. I went to school in California where my mother's people live. Mother died when I was born and my grandmother, her mother, took me when I was a baby. I was ten years old when grandmother died. I came back to Dad then. Don't you think we'd better be getting back to the ranch?'

The Running W hands, under Hatfield's direction, had thrown together a rough but comfortable cabin for Teri's use until a new ranchhouse could be built. Enough furniture was obtained in Creston to outfit it after a fashion.

'Don't worry about me,' Teri assured her

new foreman. 'I've roughed it plenty of times. Used to ride with Dad and sleep in line cabins or in the open. I'll make out fine in this. I think it's adorable, and it's amazing how quickly you built it. You seem to know all about building houses.'

Jim Hatfield, who before the death of his father at the hands of wideloopers sent him into the Rangers, had had three years at a widely known college of engineering, smiled slightly but did not otherwise reply.

The following evening Hatfield again rode to Creston. He found the town booming, for it was payday at the mines and the railroad construction camps and also at most of the spreads in the section. The boys were all in town to celebrate and they craved diversion.

Upon arriving at Creston, Hatfield immediately repaired to the railroad telegraph office. There he sent two messages that caused the operator, sworn to secrecy by the rules of his company, to regard him with curiosity and interest.

One telegram was directed to Captain Bill McDowell, Ranger Post Headquarters, Franklin. The other was to James G. Dunn, General Manager, C & P Railroad.

'I'll be back in a day or two for the answers,' Hatfield told the operator. 'Hold them for me.'

The Dust Layer was doing a roaring business and Wade Hansford, the owner, was in a complacent mood.

'Got me a new dealer to take the place of Pete Spencer,' he told Hatfield. 'He's good, too. Came in on the evening train from the west yesterday, looking for a job. I hired him as soon as he showed me what he could do with cards. Looks like a salty jigger if necessary, too. Name of Bart Cole. That's him over at the big table.'

Over the rim of his glass, Hatfield studied the new dealer. He was tall and broad shouldered with slender, muscular hands, the fingers of which were long and tapering. His face was rather pale except for a peculiar darkening at his cheek bones, and around his deep-set and extremely bright black eyes. A long jagged scar extended from just below the left corner of his mouth almost up to the cheekbone.

Strikingly in contrast to his dark eyes was his hair, which was crisply golden and inclined to curl. His mouth was firmly set, his chin jutting. He wore the conventional black garb of a gambler and wore it as if accustomed to it. His ruffled shirt front was snowy white, his black boots polished to mirror-like brightness.

'Good-looking jigger, except for that bad knife scar,' Hatfield commented. 'Acts like he knows his business. Where'd he come from?'

'Didn't say,' replied Hansford, 'and nacherly I didn't ask him. Yuh don't ask over many questions west of the Pecos, partickler of gamblers as to where they were last.'

'Isn't generally considered polite,' Hatfield admitted.

'Glad to get him without asking questions,' Hansford added. 'Looks like we're in for a big night, thanks to you.'

'Why to me?' Hatfield asked.

'Because if yuh hadn't chased them damned Death Riders away from that express car, the boys at the mine wouldn't have had any payday,' Hansford replied. 'I heard all about it. Feller, it was a fine chore yuh did, and the community owes yuh a vote of thanks for doing in those two hellions.'

He glanced about, and lowered his voice.

'And I reckon there are gents who figger *they* owe yuh something, too,' he added, 'and not thanks, either. Yuh wanta watch yore step, son, they'll be out to get yuh and they don't miss no tricks. If I was you, I'd sift sand outa this section.'

'Can't afford to,' Hatfield replied easily. 'Just signed up for a foreman's job, and foremen's jobs aren't come by every day.'

'I heard about that, too,' said Hansford, 'and I was mighty glad to hear it. Teri Wright needs a good man to help her out right now, and to keep that damn Tom Wyman from hanging around her.'

'Yuh don't think over much of Wyman?' Hatfield asked curiously.

Hansford shrugged his wide shoulders. 'Don't care over much for any sort of brand blotters,' he replied.

'Yuh figger, then, that Wyman was guilty?'

'I was on the jury that convicted him,' Hansford said. 'The evidence was plenty strong, from my way of looking at it. There was a fire with a slick iron in it, a Running W cow hawgtied on the ground and a calf cut droopy-eyed.'

'Cutting the muscles that support a calf's eyelids so they will droop closed and it can't see its mother to follow is a slick ironer's trick, all right,' Hatfield commented.

'Yeah, and Burns Wright testified that when the Running W boys rode inter sight, Wyman "waved 'em around,"' Hansford added.

'When a jigger waves his hat in a semi-circle from left to right, it means folks aren't wanted and had better stay away if they don't want to stop "hot lead"; so why didn't he start shooting when the boys kept on coming?' Hatfield asked.

'Reckon he would have, only Burns Wright rode outa the bushes behind him and got the drop on him,' Hansford countered grimly. 'Wyman contended he was just waving the boys to come and see what he'd found.'

'Which would be the nacherel thing for an honest man to do,' Hatfield pointed out.

'Uh-huh, for an *honest* man; but Wright swore it was a wave around.'

'Seemed to be some doubt in the judge's mind, from the light sentence he gave Wyman,'

Hatfield argued.

'Yes, there was,' Hansford admitted. 'One point seemed to bother the judge; he mentioned it when he charged the jury. Tom Wyman was gentling the horse he rode.'

'He was riding a horse not trained to the rope?'

'That's right. I know it looked funny for a feller to go out slick ironing on a horse that wasn't twine trained, but it's possible to rope a running cow from an untrained horse and throw it hard enough to stun it long enough to get a tie-rope on it.'

'Yes, it's possible,' Hatfield agreed.

'That's the way the jury figgered it,' Hansford said. 'But Judge Ames was bothered about that angle and Wyman got off easy because of it. He might have got off altogether if Burns Wright hadn't been close enough to be sure he "waved around" when the Running W hands came in sight.'

'In other words, it was Burns Wright's testimony that convicted him.'

'Right. And Wyman shore looked murder at Wright when he was on the witness stand. And, incidentally, it wasn't long after Wyman got outa the calaboose that Wright was done in. Funny how things work out, isn't it?'

'Yes,' Hatfield agreed cryptically. 'It is.'

The Dust Layer was filling up, and the crowd was in a boisterous and exuberant mood. Lithe young cowboys from the neighbourhood spreads, garbed in colorful range costume, rubbed shoulders with brawny miners and construction workers in red, blue or checkered shirts, corduroys and high-laced boots. There was a sprinkling of Mexican *vaqueros* in flaring velvet pantaloons, tight-fitting velvet jackets, both adorned with much silver, and steeple-crowned sombreros crusted with metal. The short skirts, shimmering with spangles, of the dance floor girls whirled in a kaleidoscope of colour as the orchestra banged out sprightly tunes. The bar was crowded three deep, the roulette wheels whirled and clicked, the faro bank was doing a record business, and all the poker tables were occupied. The clink of bottle necks on glass rims, the chink of gold pieces on the 'mahogany,' the click of dice and the silky slither of cards mingled with the babble of whirling words in a pandemonium of sound that quivered the hanging lamps. There was a bawling of song or what was intended for it, high words where an argument was in progress, the clatter of high heels and the solider thump of boots.

The scene was cheerful and gave as yet, but Hatfield sensed an undertone that might at any minute explode with dynamic violence. These were men of action, the blood running swiftly in their veins, their passions elemental. His green eyes roved constantly about the room, missing nothing, underestimating nothing, properly and precisely cataloguing every individual they rested upon. He noted several knots of quiet, watchful men who kept to themselves, drank without undue show of emotion, and were observant of all that went on around them. Almost to a man they wore riding costumes that showed signs of much usage, and they wore gun and knife in a manner that showed they were not worn as ornaments.

'Salty jiggers,' was the Lone Wolf's estimation, 'and they don't make their living twirling a rope or busting rock. Most anything's liable to happen in this town tonight.'

An argumentative poker game was in progress at the big table presided over by Bart Cole, the new dealer. Suddenly tempers flared. A young cowboy, more than half-drunk, losing a pot he had been sure of winning, grabbed the cards and tore them to bits. The dealer spoke to him in tones of quiet remonstrance.

The cowboy, his face flushing with added resentment, started up from his chair, dropping his hand to his gun belt at the same moment.

Wade Hansford, who had been watching the table, started forward, but before he had taken a step, the dealer's hand shot out. A stubby, double-barrelled derringer slid from his sleeve and spatted into his palm. The young puncher looked into the twin black muzzles, rock-steady, that yawned hungrily at him. The dealer did not speak, but the glitter in his black eyes said plenty.

The cowboy, his face whitening, sank back into his chair, sobered, all the belligerency shocked out of him. The dealer flickered a hard glance around the table; flipped the short gun back into his sleeve with a supple wrist motion and began breaking out a fresh deck of cards as if nothing had happened.

'A smooth hand, and plenty salty,' Jim Hatfield commented, apropos of the scar-faced dealer.

Wade Hansford relaxed and reached for his glass.

'Yes, a good man,' he agreed. 'I'm glad I got him.'

A few minutes later the Running W hands bulged through the swinging doors, old Stiffy Jones stumping along in the lead. They greeted Hatfield enthusiastically, crowded around him at the end of the bar and bawled for drinks.

'Whoop 'er up as high as yuh want to-night,' Hatfield told them. 'But I want every one of you work dodgers on the job to-morrow. I want every saleable beef combed outa those brakes and canyons on the north range. We'd ought get a good herd together by the end of the week.'

'We'll get 'em,' his men declared. 'Anythin' you say, Boss.'

Old Stiffy Jones was a wandering drunk. He waddled about the room, sidling up to groups, engaging table companies and dance floor girls in conversation, horning in where he had no business to be. Hatfield watched his erratic movements with a disapproving eye, but said nothing.

Finally Stiffy approached one of the quiet drinking groups at the bar and began a rambling monologue that evidently irritated the men, who were intent on their own affairs. Hatfield put down his glass and casually strolled along the bar.

Abruptly one of the individuals Stiffy was annoying with his incoherent yammerings, a burly giant of a man with craggy overhanging brows and a mouth that was a red gash across his sallow face, whirled with a curse, gripped Stiffy by the shirt collar and drew back a ponderous fist to strike the old waddie in the face. The next instant he yelled with agony as slim, bronzed fingers like rods of nickel steel closed on his wrist in a grip that ground the bones together.

'Lay off,' Jim Hatfield told him quietly, as he let go his wrist. 'He's thirty years older and fifty pounds lighter than you. I'll take him away.'

The giant let out a bellow of rage.

'But you ain't, high-pockets,' he rasped, and let drive at the Ranger.

Before the blow had travelled six inches it was blocked. The next instant something like the slim, steely face of a sledgehammer landed on the big man's jaw with a smack like a butcher's cleaver on a side of beef.

The big man apparently 'growed' wings. He shot through the air, turned over once and hit the floor with a crash that shook the rafters. For a moment he lay stunned, then he scrambled to a sitting position, howling curses through the blood that poured from his mouth and nose. His hand flickered down and up, there was a gleam of metal in the lamplight.

The room rocked to the crash of a shot. The big man howled louder than ever and gripped his blood-spouting right hand. His gun, the lock smashed by the heavy slug from Hatfield's Colt, lay half-way across the room.

Instantly the giant's companions went for their guns. Then they froze stiffly, staring into two black muzzles that seemed to single out each and everyone for individual attention.

Jim Hatfield spoke, his voice low and quiet, but carrying to every ear in the suddenly silent room.

'Step up, boys, and don't be bashful,' he said. 'I've got a trump for every trick yuh can play. Step up—don't be bashful.'

But the boys *were* 'bashful'. They didn't at all like the looks of those rock-steady gun muzzles, and the eyes the colour of snow-drifted ice behind them. They hesitated, glaring and muttering.

Hatfield gestured with a gun barrel.

'I figger yuh'll find it healthier outside,' he

said in the same quiet voice. 'Haul that fangin' sidewinder off the floor and take him with yuh—he isn't hurt bad. Get going!'

Again they hesitated for a moment, but there was an authority in those quiet tones that would not be denied. Muttering and glaring, they hauled their moaning companion from the floor and filed out, casting black looks over their shoulders as they vanished into the night.

Hatfield sheated his sixes and turned. Behind him was a bristle of guns, trained on the bar and every section of the room. The Running W hands were 'there,' ready to back to the limit any play their foreman might see fit to make.

'Thanks,' Hatfield nodded briefly. The cowboys grinned, leathered their irons and turned back to their drinks. Hatfield heard an old puncher nearby make a remark in sententious tones:

'That's a salty outfit I wouldn't want to buck up against, pertickler with that big ice-eyed hellion headin' the pack. Them guns just growed in his hands.'

'You stay put where yuh belong,' Hatfield ordered Stiffy, and was about to rejoin his riders when he noticed something black lying on the floor where the big man had fallen. He stooped and picked it up. As it turned over in his hand, he hastily crumpled it out of sight.

It was a square of black silk, cut with eyeholes and smeared with white paint, a fellow to the two death's-head masks he had taken from the faces of the dead train wreckers.

## Chapter Five

## 'CAUGHT SETTIN'

Half an hour passed. Wade Hansford moved behind the bar, emptied his money tills and placed their contents in a sack. With a nod to Hatfield, he crossed to the door of the back room and entered it, closing the door after him. A few minutes later a man bearing a bucket and mop came out of the room and sidled up to Hatfield.

'The Boss wants to see yuh a minute in the back room,' he said in low tones.

Hatfield gave him a sharp glance, nodded, and headed for the back room, the swamper padding after him. He opened the door and entered. He heard the door click shut behind him. He stiffened, staring across the room.

A single bracket lamp burned dimly on the wall. By its light, Hatfield saw Wade Hansford sitting at a table in the middle of the room, blood on his white face. On the far side of the room beside a tall iron safe stood a man with a levelled sawn-off shotgun, the twin muzzles trained on the Ranger. On the other side of the safe stood a second man, a ready six-gun in his hand. Beside the open door of the safe squatted a third man, transferring its contents to a canvas sack. All three men wore the skull masks of the Death Riders.

'Elevate!' the shotgun holder ordered harshly.

Hatfield raised both hands shoulder high.

'Set down at that table with the other feller,' the gunman said.

Hatfield obeyed—there was nothing else to do. He lowered himself into the vacant chair beside Hansford. The gunman stood motionless and alert, his eyes fixed on the Lone Wolf's raised hands. What he did not see was Hatfield's foot slowly rising under the table until his toe hooked against the far sideboard of the table.

The man at the safe finished his job, straightened up, and tightened the pucker string of his bulging sack.

'Okay,' the shotgun holder directed, 'tie that saloon-keeper and gag him. The other hellion goes with us.'

The second man holstered his Colt and started toward Hansford, fingering a short length of rope. For a moment he was almost between the shotgun holder and the table.

Jim Hatfield's foot shot forward and up with all the strength of his bent leg behind it. The table surged into the air, flipped over. Hatfield went sideways from his chair.

Both barrels of the shotgun let go with a deafening crash, but the buckshot charges slammed into the heavy table-top.

Hatfield's Colts flipped from their sheaths and streamed fire and smoke. The shotgun holder went down, his breast smashed and riddled with slugs from the Lone Wolf's sixes, his shotgun clattering to the floor. Again the Ranger's guns roared. The bulging sack thudded on the boards, its holder fell across it.

The third man managed to get his gun out and fire a shot. The bullet knocked splinters into Hatfield's face as he shot with his left-hand gun. The masked man gave a coughing grunt, whirled around and pitched headlong.

Hatfield shifted his aim with lightning speed. The bracket lamp flew to clinking fragments. Darkness blanketed the room. At the same instant he jerked the paralysed Wade Hansford from his chair.

The black window square beside the door at the end of the room blazed with light. The glass flew to fragments as lead stormed through. Hatfield heard the hiss of the bullets passing over his head. He fired twice at the gun flash, rolled over, and fired again. For a moment he lay motionless, listening intently. In the alley back of the saloon sounded the pad of running feet.

Hatfield surged erect, bounded across the room, located the end door and flung it open. Outside it was pitch dark. The sound of footsteps had ceased. He listened for a moment, then groped his way back into the room.

In the saloon beyond the door of the back room, which had evidently been locked on the outside by the fake swamper, sounded a wild pandemonium of shouts, yells and curses. Something hit the door with a prodigious crash. The lock creaked and groaned, but held. Again the door shook to the blow of a heavy object. A third blow and it crashed open, slamming back against the wall.

Into the room surged the Running W cowboys, guns out and ready.

'Hold it!' Hatfield shouted to them. 'Everything's under control.'

A white-faced bartender came hurrying in with a lighted lamp. Hatfield helped Wade Hansford to his feet. The saloon-keeper stood for a moment as if dazed, fingering a nasty cut on the side of his head.

'Somebody slammed me with a gun barrel as I lighted the lamp,' he muttered in reply to Hatfield's question. He shook his head to free it of cobwebs, glared about.

'What I'd like to know,' he said with vicious calm, 'is who unlocked that back door and left it unlocked. It's supposed to be allus locked. If I can catch the careless hellion responsible, he'll be looking for a job.'

'Where do yuh keep the key?' Hatfield asked.

'Under the papers in the money till at the end of the bar,' Hansford replied.

'See if it's there now,' Hatfield suggested.

Hansford left the room. He passed behind the bar and opened the till. A moment later he returned, his brow black as a thundercloud.

'It's not there now,' he announced, and swore a blistering oath.

'Looks like the blankety-blank-blanks had inside help,' he concluded, glaring at his assembled bartenders who glanced at one another in a bewildered and apprehensive way.

'Looks that way,' Hatfield agreed, ejecting the spent shells from his Colts and replacing them with fresh cartridges.

'Here comes the sheriff!' somebody yelled excitedly.

Sheriff Mack Bush shouldered his way through the crowd.

'Shet up!' he bellowed to the babbling throng. 'Let the fellers who know what happened do the talking.'

Hatfield told him what he knew, in terse sentences. Sheriff Bush tugged at his moustache, glared about. His gaze centred on the bodies of the masked outlaws.

'Son, yuh shore been doin' a swell job since yuh landed here,' he complimented the Ranger. 'But,' he added, 'if yuh live to get away from this section, I'll be one heap surprised.'

## Chapter Six

# HELL'S CORRAL

Sheriff Bush removed the masks from the dead outlaws. Hatfield immediately recognized them as members of the group with whom he had the run-in earlier in the evening. He questioned Hansford about the swamper who lured him into the back room.

'Sure he was one of them,' said the saloonkeeper. 'He took his mask off, picked up a mop and bucket standing in the corner, and slid out.'

'Where did he get the key with which to lock the door after he got me inter the room?' Hatfield asked.

'Outa my pocket,' replied Hansford. 'Seem to know right where to look for it, too. Funny, too, they evidently knew I'd hired several extra hands to-day to try and keep this darn place clean to-night, and that he wouldn't risk much chance of being spotted by somebody not working here. They didn't seem to miss a trick.'

A little later, Hatfield led his men, whooping and singing, hack to the Running W. Arriving at the bunkhouse, the cowboys immediately tumbled into their bunks.

But Hatfield did not go to bed for some time. Instead, he sat at the open window smoking, and reviewing the night's happenings.

‘A nervy outfit,’ he mused. ‘They knew the Dust Layer was taking in a fortune to-night. Waited until Hansford had made his midnight clean-up from the Bar and the tables and then landed on him. Had part of the outfit pull the job and the rest wait in the alley back of the saloon to take care of anybody who might happen along and to prevent interruption. Uh-huh, a smooth and salty outfit, but with a weak spot. Somebody, perhaps the boss of the gang, goes in for revenge. They figgered on evening up with me to-night. Take me along with them and do for me somewhere. Well, I’ll sure know that big hellion I busted if I ever see him again. Wonder if he’s the big skookum he-wolf of the pack? I’d say no. Looked sorta dumb. Proved it by starting that rukus with old Stiffy. No, I figger he’s just a hired hand and mebbe the weak link of the outfit.

‘That one I downed at the train wreck—the one who couldn’t keep his hands out of a dead man’s pockets,’ he added cryptically, ‘was another. *He* made me sure about what I was already suspecting.’

As the thought ran through his mind, he took from his pocket the peculiar silver rod with a ball at the end which he had taken from the dead train wrecker and examined it by the moonlight streaming through the bunkhouse window. With a nod of satisfaction he slipped it back into his pocket.

‘Uh-huh, that’s the tie-up,’ he remarked

aloud. 'But where in blazes is the jigger I've got to run down?'

Several busy days followed. Hatfield and his riders combed the brakes and canyons for saleable beefs. As the Lone Wolf suspected, they found plenty holed up in the cool gorges where there was water and shelter from the sun and rich grass. They were an ornery, intractable lot and gave plenty of trouble as windies usually do.

'Who ever named that sorta cows "windies" shore had the right notion,' Stiffy Jones declared after a long chase after a belligerent steer. 'I shore am plumb winded.'

'To-morrow we'll hit those thickets to the west and see if we can't run out a few cedar-breakers,' Hatfield said.

Old Stiffy gave a groan.

'If there's a wuss chore than snakin' ladino cows outa cedar thickets, I don't know what it is!' he complained.

'Yuh'd oughta try bustin' "sea lion" cows down in the coast country like I did once,' a young cowboy remarked gravely. 'Them sea lion cows come right up outa the Gulf of Mexico. They got fins on their hocks and when yuh drop a loop on 'em, they raise up a foot and saw the rope in two with a fin.'

'Son,' old Stiffy replied severely, 'lyin' to a man of my age ain't decent. Them sea lion cows don't have no fins on their hocks. They have 'em on the end of their tails. They cut the twine by wrappin' their tail around it and givin' a quick jerk. You stick to the truth hereafter and folks will think better of yuh.'

The following day, Hatfield rode to town and visited the telegraph office. There was no reply from his message to Captain McDowell, but there was one from General Manager Dunn, of the C & P. It was laconic and cryptic, but Hatfield chuckled as he read it and looked pleased.

'*Bring them in*,' was all it said.

Jim Hatfield took another ride. In the dark hours before the dawn, he and old Stiffy Jones quietly left the Running W spread and headed south-west.

'I want to go over the route we'll use to run that herd to the construction camp,' Hatfield told the old waddie.

'Only one trail we can use,' said Stiffy. 'That's by way of White Horse Canyon. It's the only way yuh can get through the Embrujada Hills with a herd. A horse can't get across that upended section of hell by any other way. Plumb outa the question for beefs. Yeah, we'll hafta use White Horse Canyon and she's a heller.'

Dawn was streaking the sky when they entered the canyon in question. Hatfield was soon ready to agree with Stiffy that it was a 'heller'. It was as if some flaming sword of vengeance had cloven the hills to leave the awful gorge with its towering splintered walls and its gloomy, boulder-strewn floor. So rugged and stony was the floor of the canyon that practically no growth could find rootage in the scanty soil. Waterless, barren, the mighty cleft bored into the frowning, craggy hills that were themselves a scene of arid desolation.

'One good thing about it, though,' Hatfield commented. 'There isn't a place for a widelooping outfit to hole up. I've a hunch the Death Riders would like to take a try at us. That big herd is a temptation to any widelooping gang, and from what I've learned those hellions seem to have a pick on the Running W for some reason or other.'

'Uh-huh,' agreed Stiffy, 'it looks that way.'

Mile after mile they rode, with the rock walls of the gorge slowly drawing together until the canyon was but a narrow defile swathed in this gloom. High overhead was a narrow thread of blue sky pressing down upon the jagged, splintered rim. No bush or vine clung to the precipitous walls, but here and there hung long streamers of sad-hued lichens like the grizzled beard on a dead man's chin. No bird sang in the sombre depths, there was no cheerful ripple of water, no sprightly rustle of leaf or branch under the caress of the wind. The gloom was thick and oppressive. Only the heavier dregs of light reached the rocky floor. No bright-winged sunbeam could fall so far. They died far, far above.

They had covered perhaps half the distance

between the Running W and the construction camp when they saw the first break in the grim barriers of stone. To the left yawned a narrow side canyon thickly grown with tall growth. On the far side of the narrow trail the growth continued, crowding up against the west wall of the main canyon and extending up and down it for several hundred yards before it petered out in a thin straggle that was quickly replaced by the scattering of monotonous boulders.

Hatfield pulled Goldy to a halt and stared at the brush-choked mouth of the side canyon.

'If they try it anyplace, it'll be here, or I'm a heap mistook,' he said. 'Let's take a look at that hole over there.'

With difficulty they pushed their mounts through the thick brush that filled the mouth of the narrower gorge. For perhaps a hundred feet the bushes grew closely together and higher than the head of a mounted man, their tops interlacing to form a tangle of greyish-green. Then gradually the growth became thinner until it almost ceased altogether in the centre of the gorge, although it still grew thick along the walls.

Hatfield uttered a sharp exclamation. Down the centre of the gorge ran a trail, little more than a game track. And scarring its surface were prints of both horses' irons and cattle hoofs.

'Somebody used this hole-in-the-wall,' he

muttered. 'Wonder where it leads to?'

'I'd figger it runs out on to the desert to the east,' hazarded Stiffy. 'Ain't never rode through it. Didn't figger anybody else ever had. Sure nothin' to make anybody want to, so far as I can see.'

'Nor so far as anybody else could see,' Hatfield admitted. But it's sure as shooting that somebody has ridden this way.'

He dismounted and studied the hoof marks closely.

'Been used going and coming,' he announced. 'The prints point both ways.'

'Some kind of a short cut to somewhere,' Stiffy guessed. 'Them prints don't look pertickler fresh.'

'Week or more old,' Hatfield agreed. 'Well, let's get back to White Horse and see if there's any other likely place between here and the camp.'

They continued to follow the winding gorge until the hills fell back and the canyon ended. They found themselves on the crest of a long sag that sloped gently downward to a scene of activity.

East and west stretched the range of hills. At their base a shimmer of steel flowed out of the east. Stiffy gestured to it.

'There's the railroad line,' he said. 'It curves around the hills from the north-east. There's the camp right down below, and further on yuh can see where they're drivin' a cut and a tunnel through the hills to get to the desert on the other side. They can't get straight south around the hills because they can't get across the gorge on the other side of the Rio Grande. They gotta skirt that gorge and cross a long ways to the west. That's why they're drivin' the cut here.'

Hatfield nodded, his eyes on the bustling camp below. A mile or more to the south loomed the bristle of crags thrust out from the main body of the hills to the west. He could see the dark mouth of the cut, from which rose plumes of steam. The camp itself was a widespread straggle of shacks and temporary buildings, with long lines of camp cars standing on sidings. Other sidings were occupied by cars loaded with materials, which puffing locomotives shifted back and forth.

'They got a good-sized yard down there,' he mused.

'Uh-huh,' Stiffy agreed. 'I understand that's gonna be permanent. A distributing yard for the east and west traffic comin' up over the southbound line. See—they're buildin' shops and a roundhouse and office buildin's. Over there to the right is the cattle yard. Nothin' much in it right now. I've a notion they'll be plumb glad to see our beefs, only I'm scairt they won't buy 'em. It's been the road's policy to buy only from shippers who contract with 'em for a steady supply.'

Hatfield smiled slightly, but said nothing.

'Goin' down to the camp?' Stiffy asked.

Hatfield shook his head. 'Nope,' he said. 'Don't want to be seen down there. We're headed back around the hills to the east, not through the canyon. Our business is to keep outa sight.'

'It'll be plumb dark before we get home,' Stiffy replied in disgusted tones.

'So much the better,' Hatfield said. 'Let's go.'

It was, in truth, long after dark when they reached the spread after an arduous ride.

'That side canyon mouth is the only place there'd be a chance of pulling something,' Hatfield remarked to Stiffy as they got the rigs off their weary horses. 'It's a perfect set-up, too. The canyon is so narrow there and so choked with brush that the point, swing and flank riders will hafta pull in and join up with the drag riders behind the herd. The whole outfit will be bunched up in the rear of the herd when they're passing that canyon. Yuh'll hafta be on yore toes, Stiffy, and yuh'll be taking a chance of stopping lead. Willing to risk it?'

'The bullet ain't run what can do for me,' old Stiffy declared grimly. 'Right now I got so much lead in my carcass it would pay to mine me. The only time I was ever in any real danger of cashin' in was once when I had so many bullet holes in me I like to starved to death from leakin' out my vittles.'

Jim Hatfield harboured a faint suspicion that Stiffy Jones' statements were not generally believed.

The morning of the second day after their ride through the canyon, the herd got under way. It was a big herd, bigger than even Hatfield had dared to hope for, and the beefs were in prime condition.

'With the money those cows will bring, yuh'll be sitting purty for quite a spell,' Hatfield told Teri Wright the night before the drive.

South by west rolled the welter of shaggy backs and tossing horns that was the shipping herd. Point men rode near its head to direct the course of the herd. About a third of the way back from the point men were the swing riders where the herd began to bend in case of a change of course. Another third of the way back were the flank riders whose duty was to block the cattle from sidewise wandering.

Bringing up the drag were the tail or drag riders who had the most disagreeable of all the chores. They were exposed to the dust raised by the entire herd and had their patience sorely tried by the slow or obstinate animals that continually fell back to the rear of the herd.

As the drag was a short one, there was no remuda and no chuck-wagon. Ordinarily Stiffy Jones, the trail boss, would have ridden far ahead of the herd to survey the ground and search out watering places and good grazing ground. But with the expectation of ringing the herd to its destination before nightfall these duties were not necessary and Stiffy rode with the drag men behind the herd.

Stiffy had with him only about half of the Running W outfit. The others aimed with rifle and revolver, Jim Hatfield at their head, had ridden away from the spread during the dark hours of the night before, circling through the north hills to reach the black mouth of White Horse Canyon.

Old Stiffy was watchful and alert, his heavy rifle rested across his saddle bow and his keen old eyes constantly searched the terrain on either side of the ambling cattle. His riders were also tense and expectant and there was little of the chaff and skylarking that usually is part of the beginning of a trail. The Running W cowboys knew they were taking their lives in their hands if their foreman's suspicions should prove correct, and their mood was correspondingly serious.

Into White Horse Canyon flowed the herd, not liking it at all and bawling protest at the gloom and the hard going. It took considerable urging on the part of the riders to keep the cows going. They showed a tendency to mill, but the point riders herded in those attempting to fan out on either side and the drag men forced the stragglers to keep up with the main body.

Darker and darker grew the gorge and

nearer and nearer the black cliffs drew together. The querulous bellowing of the cattle echoed drearily from the towering walls. Their hoofs drummed loudly on the rocky floor.

The cowboys crouched low in their saddles, peering ahead, tense and expectant. The gloom increased.

The head of the herd reached the ominous side canyon mouth, flowed past it. The main body jostled on with tossing heads and rolling eyes. The riders crouched lower in their saddles. The point, swing and flank riders had dropped back until the whole outfit was riding behind the herd, keeping as far apart as possible, shielding themselves behind their horses' necks. They gripped the bridles with sweating palms and strained their eyes ahead.

With nerve-shattering unexpectedness the 'expected' happened. Shots boomed from the brush-choked canyon mouth. Lead hissed about the Running W riders. With one accord they whirled their horses and raced madly back the way they had come. The herd bawled with terror and began to mill.

Out of the brush streamed masked men, hooting derisively as they hurled bullets after the fleeing cowboys. their whoops of triumph changed to howls of terror as from the dark thicket on the far side of the trail burst a blaze of gunfire. Under that first thunderous volley three saddles were emptied. The survivors fought madly to turn their frantic horses. They fired wildly at the growth where nothing moved but from which that storm blast of death continued to pour.

Two more wideloopers went down. Another screamed with pain as a bullet smashed his arm. His companions fled madly for the shelter of the side canyon.

Last of all was a tall man on a splendid black horse. With word and gesture he urged his men to cover. Coolly he turned in the saddle and sent a stream of bullets towards the thicket.

Jim Hatfield threw down on the tall leader. His green eyes gleamed as he pulled trigger. He saw the tall bandit sway in his saddle, but before he could fire again the outlaw leader had vanished into the protective screen of the growth.

'After the hellions!' thundered the Lone Wolf. His men pounding after him, he raced to where their horses were tethered some little distance off in the brush. The Running W riders who had staged the ambush mounted in furious haste and charged from the thicket. Immediately they were engulfed in the milling herd. It took minutes to disentangle themselves from the terrified cattle.

Old Stiffy and the hands who had trailed the herd came racing back, whooping with excitement.

'Take the herd on to the camp!' Hatfield shouted to them as he led his party into the growth. They tore through the brush, heedless of thorns and whipping branches. When they bulged from the final straggle of bushes, there was no sight of the dry-gulchers.

'Only one way for them to go,' Hatfield cried. 'After them!'

Neck and neck the party thundered down the canyon, which soon began to curve. Hatfield spoke a word of caution.

'Easy,' he said. 'They've got a start on us and we can't run them down in a hurry. Our best bet will be when they hit the open desert beyond the canyon mouth. Easy, and look out. They might hole up and lay for us around one of these turns. We don't wanta ride inter a trap.'

At a swift pace he led his men, but as the canyon narrowed and the turns became more frequent, he slowed them down.

Mile after mile they rode, watchful, alert, peering and listening. The canyon had narrowed until the east and west walls were less than a hundred yards apart. The perpendicular rock walls were replaced by brush-covered slopes that stretched upward to the torn and jagged rimrock far above. On the left the brush-grown slope was fairly gentle, but on the right it soared steeply upward, bristling with chaparral, studded with boulders. The canyon also was choked with dead-looking growth between which the trail ran so narrow that they were forced to proceed in single file.

So ominous, indeed, was the terrain that Hatfield slowed the pursuit to a walk.

Suddenly he uttered an exclamation and reined in. Directly ahead of them a cloud of smoke was boiling up.

'The hellions have fired the brush to hold us off,' he rasped.

One of his cowboys let out a yell.

'There's smoke comin' up behind us, too!' he bawled.

Hatfield glanced back the way they had come. There, too, was a billowing, yellowish cloud.

'We're trapped!' yammered the cowboy who had first sighted the smoke behind them. 'We'll be roasted alive.'

'Shut up!' Hatfield told him. 'We're not done yet, but we've gotta move fast. This brush is dry as tinder and there's a wind blowing. We've got to make it up the slope to the rimrock.'

'Come on!' shouted the cowboy, and turned his horse's head to the left.

But Jim Hatfield's long arm shot out and seized his bridle in an iron grip.

'Not that way, yuh damn fool!' he exclaimed. 'That's the easy way—the way they figger us to take. Ride up that slope and we'll be shot down like settin' brush hens! Turn to the right.'

'We can't ever make it up that straight-up-and-down sag!' wailed another rider.

'Yuh'll make it or burn before the Resurrection

Day!' Hatfield told him grimly. 'Get going! That fire's coming fast, both ways.'

Up the steep sag they sent their horses, the animals slipping and floundering and giving protesting snorts. Already the smoke was drifting about them in acrid clouds. They could hear the crackle and roar of the flames as it tore through the dry growth, fanned by a strong cross wind. As they got farther up the slope they could see that the canyon to the north and south was a seething welter of fire which was crawling swiftly up the slope and threatening to cut them off before they could reach the sanctuary of the rimrock.

Faster and faster scrambled the now thoroughly terrified horses, their riders urging them on to greater efforts with voice and spur, but faster still the fire narrowed the already dangerously narrow lane of escape.

They reached a point that was comparatively free of growth, studded with boulders and composed largely of loose shale that rolled and slipped under the horses' hoofs. Something sang over their heads and spattered against a stone.

'Good God!' somebody yelled. 'They're shooting at us!'

Goldy could have easily outstripped the other horses and borne his rider to safety, but Hatfield held him firmly in check and kept to the rear of his men, encouraging the weaker, herding the stragglers towards the easiest route. Now he turned in the saddle, stared over his shoulder and slipped to the ground, sliding his Winchester from the boot as he did so. Bracing his back against a boulder, he gazed across the smoke-filled canyon to the far slope. The fierce draught raging down the gorge held the smoke clouds low and the visibility was fairly good.

A bullet spatted viciously against the stone scant inches from his head, showering him with stinging fragments. Without moving, he continued to stare across the canyon.

Another bullet hit the stone, but this time the Lone Wolf's keen eyes spotted the tell-tale whitish puff that rose from the growth. The Winchester leaped to his shoulder, his steady eyes glanced along the sights. Shot after shot he poured into the brush beneath the smoke-puff.

At the fourth shot, the growth was violently agitated. Something black pitched from it and rolled down the slope. Hatfield still stood tense and motionless, watching and waiting.

No more slugs whined across the smoke-filled gorge. The growth remained silent.

'Just one of 'em climbed up there to keep a look-out,' he muttered as he turned and flung himself into the saddle. Holstering his rifle, he sent Goldy speeding after his companions who were now far ahead.

The heat was stifling, the smoke so thick he could hardly breathe. His ears rang to the roar of the conflagration. Straining his eyes ahead, he suddenly saw a tongue of flame waver directly in front of him. It vanished, was supplanted by another and broader. Then the growth ahead was displaced by a flickering wall of fire. The flames had closed the gap.

Hatfield bent low in the saddle, shielding his face with his arms. His voice rang out:

'Trail, Goldy! Trail!'

With a scream of pain and terror, the great sorrel plunged into the curtain of flame. Hatfield gasped as the fiery fingers bit at his flesh. The breath was stopped in his throat. His temples throbbed, his chest constricted. All around him roared and crackled the burning brush. Hot brands showered down upon him, his nostrils were choked by clouds of stinging ash. He felt Goldy stagger, reel, flounder as his hoofs slipped on the stones. He held him to his footing with an iron grip on the reins, called hoarse encouragement.

Another mighty effort, an explosive snort from the great sorrel, and the fire was behind him. Through the swirling smoke he could see his hands urging the horses up the rimrock, casting anxious glances over their shoulders. They yelled with delight as their foreman burst through the final fringe of fire and into sight. A moment more and Hatfield was beside them beating out the fire that smouldered his garments. On top of the rimrock, with the fire raging below them, they pulled up in comparatively clear air. Hatfield stared down into the inferno that was the canyon.

'Well,' he said, 'they took that trick, and they almost played trumps against us, but they didn't get the herd.'

'And they didn't get us, either,' exulted a cowboy; 'but just the same I figger to eat my chuck raw from here on. I don't wanta ever see another fire!'

## Chapter Seven

## MURDER

Goldy had lost some patches of hair and Hatfield part of his clothes. He also had a few blisters on his hands. The Running W riders were smoke-blackened and red-eyed and some had sustained slight burns from flying brands. But aside from these minor discomforts, nobody was the worse for their harrowing experience. Hatfield grinned as he surveyed his grimy crew.

'I've a notion we can make it along the rimrock to the south and reach the slope above the camp,' he said. 'Let's get going. I could do with a drink of water about now.'

It was long past dark, however, when after an exhausting scramble along the rimrock and down the long southern slopes of the hills they reached the construction camp. Hatfield at once repaired to the office of the stockyard superintendent where he found old Stiffy anxiously awaiting him.

'Didn't have a mite of trouble the rest of the way,' Stiffy told him. 'Son, yuh shore give them hellions a bellyful. We looked over the three that were downed there in the canyon mouth. Mean lookin' cusses, but nobody recognized any of 'em. Death Riders, all right, or at least they wore them damn painted masks. I brung the masks along in case yuh'd like to have 'em.'

The stockyard superintendent was glad to get the herd.

'Prime steers, all of 'em,' he said. 'We needed 'em. These rockbusters won't work without plenty of whisky and meat. I got 'em all weighed up and here's a voucher made out for yuh. Yuh can cash it at the office in Creston. Say, you must have a stand with the Old Man—Jaggers Dunn, the General Manager. We got word from him the other day to buy every head yuh brought in. That's the fust time he agreed to accept stuff in small lots without any guarantee of further shipments. Do yuh know him puhsonal?'

'I worked with him once,' Hatfield replied, not considering it necessary to add that the great General Manager of the C & P looked upon him as one of his closest personal friends.

The Running W outfit, somewhat burned and battered, but otherwise none the worse for the day's adventures, headed back to camp early the following morning. Hatfield, after pausing at the spread for food and a change of clothing, proceeded to Creston where he cashed the voucher received for the herd and deposited it to Teri Wright's account. Late in the evening, he entered the Dust Layer in search of something to eat and found Wade Hansford regarding his new dealer, Bart Cole, with a dissatisfied eye.

'Look at the hellion,' he told Hatfield.

Observing the dealer, Hatfield noted that Cole's face was pasty coloured, his hands shook and he manipulated the cards in a clumsy fashion decidedly in contrast to his former smooth dealing.

'The sidewinder took the day off yesterday, and like all of 'em he went on a bat,' Hansford declared in disgusted tones. 'He was sober, all right, when he showed up for work this evening, but he's got the jerks. Handles the pasteboards like his arm was broke and don't seem to have his mind on his business.'

Hatfield eyed the dealer thoughtfully but did not comment.

Two days later, Hatfield received an answer to his telegram to Captain Bill McDowell in charge of the Ranger post at Franklin. The first part of the message brought a leaping glow to his green eyes, but the second half was unsatisfactory. For some minutes Hatfield studied the terse sentences which stated:

'No trace found of man such as you describe. Arizona and New Mexico authorities know nothing of anybody answering said description.'

The result of Hatfield's minutes of hard thinking was another and longer message to the Ranger Captain.

* * *

Tom Wyman was a frequent visitor at the Running W. The Running W hands received him without comment, with the exception of old Stiffy Jones who was querulous.

'I figger it ain't showin' much respect for the dead Boss,' Stiffy complained to Hatfield. 'Burns Wright's testimony at the trial was what convicted Wyman, you know. I don't know whether Wyman was guilty or not, scein' as I wasn't there and didn't see what happened, but I know Burns was allus shore Wyman was guilty. He swore he saw Wyman wave the boys around, and I don't see how he coulda been mistook seein' as he was right behind him.'

'He and Wyman had trouble before, hadn't they?' Hatfield asked.

'I don't know as yuh could call it trouble,' Stiffy objected. 'Burns didn't like him hangin' around Miss Teri and told her so. He never said anythin' to Wyman about it so far as I know.'

'Why did he object to Wyman seeing Miss

Teri?' Hatfield asked.

Stiffy shrugged his shoulders.

'Well,' he said, 'Wyman was a sorta hell raiser—salty young jigger and kinda on the prod. He used to drink and gamble quite a bit, too.'

'*Used to?* When did he stop?'

'After he started coming to see Miss Teri,' Stiffy admitted, 'but yuh never can tell about that sort. I reckon Burns figgered he was liable to bust loose again. After all, he was her uncle, and it was his chore to look after her when her dad cashed in.'

Hatfield was silent for a moment, then suddenly he asked an apparently irrelevant question:

'How old was Burns Wright?'

'About thirty-eight, I figger, mebbe a year or two older—just a young feller,' Stiffy replied.

Hatfield looked thoughtful, but said nothing.

Two days later, Tom Wyman was again the subject of conversation between Jim Hatfield and Stiffy Jones. Stiffy had just ridden in from town.

'Came nigh onto bein' trouble in the Dust Layer this afternoon,' the garrulous old waddie said. 'Tom Wyman come in, and Wade Hansford told him he'd take it kind if he'd stay outa his place. For a minute I thought Wyman was gonna go for him. He looked plumb pizen. But he turned around and walked out without a word. Reckon he didn't care to tangle with Hansford. Wade is a cold proposition.'

All of which gave Hatfield considerable to think about. He was thinking about both conversations with Stiffy the following morning when he was riding to Creston to meet Teri Wright at the bank. Teri had ridden to town a couple of hours earlier, Hatfield having been detained at the spread on routine matters. There was to be a conference at the bank between Teri, old Banks Buster, owner of the Circle J, and the bank officials, and Teri wished her foreman to be present.

It was a lovely summer morning. The sun shining slantwise through the trees threw delicate traceries across the trail, with bars of golden light between. The green boughs, before and behind, shot their broad arches across the winding track. Far to the south, the desert was a shimmer of molten bronze flecked with jet where chimney rocks and isolated spires flung up like monuments set by the hand of man instead of being what they were, hoary tombstones to ages long dead. The long slopes to the crest of the hills were a myriad shades of green. Only the hum of insects and the rustle of the breeze in the leaves disturbed the silence—the sweet, restful silence of nature.

Then abruptly the silence was broken. Hatfield raised his head at the sharp clicking sound coming from somewhere ahead. Swiftly the sound swelled until it was the frantic drumming of the irons of a horse ridden at top speed.

The Ranger lost his easy slouch in the saddle. He sat tense and erect, the thumb of one slim hand hooked over his cartridge belt and close to the heavy gun swinging low on his muscular thigh. His green eyes narrowed slightly, peering watchfully ahead. There was something purposeful and urgent in the sound of those drumming hoofs so swiftly advancing to meet him. An instant longer and the rider bulged around a bend in the trail directly ahead and jerked the snorting horse to a slithering halt.

It was Teri Wright. Her eyes were wild, her face white.

'Jim!' she cried. 'I was coming for you! You're the only one I know to turn to for help!'

'Easy,' Hatfield told her. 'Catch yore breath. What's the matter? What do yuh need help about?'

'It's Tom!' she gasped. 'He's been arrested—for murder!'

Hatfield stared at the frantic girl.

'Take it easy, Teri,' he counselled again. 'For the murder of whom?'

'Of Wade Hansford.'

'Wade Hansford killed! How'd it happen?'

Under the influence of the Lone Wolf's quiet voice, the girl regained somewhat of her composure.

'It happened last night—right after dark,'

she told him. 'In the alley back of the saloon. A scream was heard and when men rushed out to see what was going on, they found Wade Hansford lying on his face with a knife in his back. And—and Tom was standing over him!'

Hatfield's face hardened, his black brows drew together.

'They had trouble yesterday,' he muttered. 'What did Tom have to say?'

'I couldn't get to see him,' Teri replied, 'but old Moreman Miller, the jailer, told me Tom said he heard a cry for help as he was passing the alley mouth—the saloon is just a couple of doors from the corner, you know, and when he went into the alley to investigate he found Hansford lying on the ground and nobody else in sight. Miller said nobody believes him.'

'The charge won't stand up in co'ht if Tom can get some support for his story.' Hatfield comforted her. 'Just being there isn't proof that he did the killing. Plenty is liable to come out before the case gets to co'ht. Yuh don't need to be so worried.'

'That's not what's worrying me!' Teri cried. 'I know Tom is innocent. There's a mob forming to lynch him!'

'The sheriff won't stand for that,' Hatfield replied.

'The sheriff isn't in town,' Teri answered. 'He and his deputies rode to the Bar H yesterday afternoon. The Death Riders rustled a herd on the Bar H yesterday morning.

There's nobody to protect the jail except old Moreman and he's past seventy years old and crippled.'

Jim Hatfield's face turned bleak as the granite scarring the hillside. His eyes seemed to subtly change colour until they were an icy grey—the grey of a stormy winter sea. He gathered up his reins.

'Be seeing yuh, Teri—don't worry,' he said. 'Trail, Goldy!'

Instantly the great sorrel shot forward, his hoofs beating a drumroll of sound. Teri Wright whirled her horse and started in pursuit, but the great golden horse drew away from her as if her speeding mount was standing still. She had a last glimpse (of a flowing back tail as Goldy whisked around a bend) and vanished. When she herself reached the bend and rounded it, although there was a long stretch of straight trail ahead, the racing sorrel and his towering rider were nowhere in sight.

## CHAPTER EIGHT

## KILL ME

In Creston, the broad street and a vacant lot fronting the jail was black with men. Foremost of the mob was a dark-eyed giant of a man with a sallow face and craggy, overhanging brows.

Across the back of his right hand was the livid scar of a newly healed wound.

Standing before the jail door, his pegleg planted solidly, was white-haired Moreman Miller. The old jailer held a gun in his one good hand.

'Come on, old man, stand aside and give us them keys!' shouted the giant with the scarred hand.

'Yuh won't get 'em,' quavered old Moreman. 'I ain't got 'em on me and I won't tell yuh where they're hid. Yuh better get away from here. The sheriff will be along any minute now.'

'To hell with the sheriff!' shouted the other. 'We're gonna string that murderin' hellion up. Yuh'll tell us where the keys are after yuh get a taste of fire on yore feet.'

'None of that, feller,' cautioned a rangy cowboy nearby. 'Nobody's gonna hurt that old jigger. We got somethin' that'll open the door. Come on, boys!'

There was a concerted rush. Moreman Miller managed to fire one shot with his shaky old hand before they closed on him, but the bullet went wild. In an instant he was disarmed and brushed aside. But a quick search of his person did not reveal the keys.

'Oh, to hell with them,' growled the big man. 'Bring that log along and get busy.'

Half a dozen men pushed to the front. They bore a heavy beam which they intended to use as a battering ram on the door.

'All together, now!' boomed the big man. 'Let 'er go!'

The end of the beam, propelled by sturdy muscles, hit the door with a thundering crash. The stout barrier creaked and groaned, but withstood their efforts. Again they hurled the beam at it. One of the planks split from top to bottom. The mob howled in triumph.

Back came the beam again, and again it crashed home. Another plank splintered. The door sagged on its loosened hinges.

'Give 'er a good one this time and it'll do it!' yelled the big man. 'Way back, and get a good start. Put yore backs behind it.'

The battering crew drew back a dozen paces from the door, got set for a running rush. The mob whooped with excitement.

The exultant whoops changed to yells of alarm as there was a roar of hoofbeats and a great golden horse tore through their ranks, scattering men right and left, bowling others over. There was a wild rush to get out of the way.

With the horse still going at full speed, his tall rider leaped from the saddle, rocked back on his heels and kept his balance by a miracle of agility. He bounded forward, seized the battering ram and tore it from its holders as if it had been a straw in a baby's hand. He hurled it from him a good dozen feet and stepped back, facing the mob.

The rising yell of fury suddenly stilled as the leaders stared into the yawning black muzzles of two rock-steady guns. Jim Hatfield spoke, his voice ringing out like the blast of a golden bugle:

'We've had enough of this damn foolishness. Disperse, and go about yore business in an orderly manner. Have yuh all gone plumb loco?'

For an instant there was stunned silence. It was broken by the craggy-browed giant's howl of wrath.

'Who the hell are you to come here and tell folks what to do?'

Instantly one of the black gun muzzles moved a trifle until it was lined with the giant's broad breast. Hatfield spoke again.

'This time,' he said, 'it won't be a crease across yore hand!'

The man who had tried to smash old Stiffy's face in the Dust Layer stood rigid. He wet his suddenly dry lips with his tongue. The colour drained from his face and he seemed to shrivel under the bleak glare of the terrible eyes behind that frowning gun muzzle.

But the rest of the mob were coming out of their bewilderment. Voices began to yell:

'What's the matter up there in front?'

'Get goin'!'

'He's only one man!'

'Kill him!'

For the third time the Lone Wolf spoke, his

voice carrying clearly to the outskirts of the mob, his tones searing with contempt.

'Kill me! It oughta be easy. There are enough of yuh—a hundred to one. But don't make any mistake. I'll get five or six of yuh before I go down. Who aims to be the fust?'

The yells and curses continued, but now they held an uncertain note. The towering man with the level green eyes had made them a fair proposition, if they wanted to take him up on it. Sure they could kill him. One shot would do it . . . Too close to miss. But—they hesitated. What he had said was gospel truth. Half a dozen men, maybe more, would go down before those flaming guns before he crumpled to the earth. Who would be the half dozen? Each man had an uneasy presentiment that he was singled out for special attention. Particularly those in the front ranks. Almost unconsciously, they began to edge back.

But those behind didn't care to change places with them. They also began to retreat, slowly at first, with greater speed as the leaders threatened to get behind them. The front line grew ragged, the fringes of the mob dissolved as men furtively edged towards the side streets. Hatfield had a glimpse of the craggy-browed giant ducking furtively out of sight. His eyes were grimly speculative as he watched the man vanish.

The mob was swiftly breaking up. After all, there wasn't much sense to this business.

There was a law in the land. It would take care of Wade Hansford's killer. Why take a chance on stopping hot lead? That big jigger meant just what he said. He was ready to die—no doubt about that. Were they? Well, not just yet! More than one man began asking himself:

'How the hell did *I* come to get into this thing, anyhow?'

The compact mob had become small, hesitant groups that shot furtive glances at the grim figure towering before the jail door. They edged still further away.

And then there was a clatter of hoofs and Sheriff Mack Bush and his deputies rode around the corner, dusty, travel-stained, weary, and evidently already in a very bad temper. The old peace officer took in the situation at a glance. He jerked his horse to a halt and swung down from the saddle, his moustache bristling in a face scarlet with anger.

'What the hell's goin' on here?' he roared. 'Why, yuh cowardly blankety-blank-blanks! Get goin', every one of yuh. If there's a man in sight in one minute, I'll lock him up for incitin' a riot and I'll make the charge stick. Move, I said!'

They moved. In considerably less than one minute the street in front of the jail was vacant. Sheriff Bush, with a final glare around, strode up to Jim Hatfield who had holstered his guns and was rolling a cigarette with the slim fingers of his left hand.

'I don't know how yuh did it, son, but it was a mighty fine chore,' the sheriff said. 'How in blazes did this thing get started? There weren't no talk of lynchin' when I rode outa town last night or I'd have took precautions. Somebody musta done some fast and hard talkin'. I wish I knowed who it was. This beats anythin' I ever, heerd tell of!

'Unlock the door, Moreman,' he added to old Miller who had ambled up, rubbing a bruised arm. 'We'll go inside and talk this over. Where's the key?'

The jailer chuckled, unstrapped his wooden leg and deftly removed the key from the padded hollow into which the stump of his limb fitted.

'Didn't think they'd figger to look there,' he said as he strapped the peg back into place and fitted the key in the lock.

Together with Trout Mason, the chief deputy, they entered the jail office. The sheriff ordered the other deputies to patrol the town and break up any gatherings that appeared threatening.

In answer to the sheriff's questioning, old Moreman Miller gave an account of what had happened before the jail.

'This big cowboy got here just in time,' Miller concluded. 'They'd have had Wyman in another minute, and he'd have been a gone goslin'. Them fellers were mighty hot, but this feller cooled 'em down pronto.'

'A fine chore,' nodded the sheriff. 'I'm mighty glad yuh happened along, Hatfield, pertickler under the circumstances.'

Hatfield shot the old peace officer a keen glance, but Bush did not see fit to elaborate.

In the meanwhile, Trout Mason, the deputy, had been eyeing Hatfield with perplexed interest. On his face was the expression of a man who is trying hard to call something to mind. Suddenly his eyes snapped with excitement. He half rose from his seat, then sank back without speaking. He continued to stare at the Ranger.

Hatfield asked an abrupt question.

'Sheriff,' he said, 'just what was Wade Hansford doing back in that alley after dark?'

The sheriff hesitated, then apparently made up his mind to something.

'He was takin' a short cut to the bank,' he replied.

'To the bank! Does the bank keep open all night in this *pueblo*?'

'Nope,' the sheriff said soberly, 'but Hansford had a meetin' there with Bulkley, the cashier.'

Hatfield regarded the old peace officer thoughtfully for a full minute.

'Sheriff,' he said in his slow, deep voice, 'are there any unusual angles to this case?'

Again the sheriff hesitated. He seemed reluctant to discuss the matter. But there was something about this tall, level-eyed cowboy that overbore his reluctance and forced him to comply with Hatfield's request.

'Yes,' he said, 'there is. Tom Wyman may have trouble provin' his innocence, but just the same I don't figger he's guilty of the killin'.'

'Not guilty?' exclaimed old Miller.

'Nope, I don't figger he is,' repeated the sheriff, and made an apparently irrelevant statement:

'Yuh see, Wade Hansford sold the Dust Layer yesterday afternoon.'

'Sold the Dust Layer!'

'Uh-huh, that's right. Sold it to a feller named Releford who'd been dickerin' with him for the place. Wade wanted to get outa the business and go back to the Nueces country where he come from. Releford made him a good offer and he took it up. Releford paid spot cash—twenty thousand dollars in gold.'

'Whe-ew!' exclaimed Trout Mason. 'That's a heap of dinero in one chunk!'

'Uh-huh, it was,' said Bush. 'That's why Hansford had a meetin' with Bulkley at the bank. He wanted that money put in the vault. Didn't like to leave it in his safe overnight, not after what happened there when Hatfield busted up the attempted robbery.' He paused, then added impressively:

'And when they picked Hansford up in the alley, just a coupla minutes after they heerd him yell, he didn't have that money on him. And—*Tom Wyman didn't have it on him either!*'

His hearers stared at him as the significance of the statement sank in.

'Mebbe he did have it and throwed it away,' hazarded Trout Mason.

'If he did, he throwed it so far nobody could find it and we looked over every inch of that alley and all around it,' grunted Bush.

'Begins to look sorta like somebody got to Hansford before Wyman,' Jim Hatfield commented.

'Uh-huh—the jigger who stuck a knife inter pore Wade's back,' replied the sheriff. 'Now you fellers understand, I don't want any of this to get outside this office. What I'm tellin' yuh is strictly confidential. I don't figger many folks knowed about Hansford havin' that money. Not even Bulkley knowed what Hansford wanted to see him about at the bank. Hansford told me, and I figgered on walkin' to the bank with him, but that trouble busted loose up at the Bar H. I reckon that's why Wade waited until dark and then snuk out the back door. Figgered it would be safer, the chances are. But somebody had an eye on him and was waitin' when he come out.'

'Looks that way,' Hatfield said. The others nodded agreement.

'Glad I ain't got no money,' remarked Moreman Miller. 'Seems of late anybody what gets his hands on a passel of *dinero* is due to take the big jump. Fust Burns Wright and now pore Wade Hansford. Twenty thousand dollars

’pears to be a sorta unlucky number. They both had twenty thousand when it happened, didn’t they?’

‘That’s right,’ nodded the sheriff.

Hatfield smoked thoughtfully for a few minutes.

‘Let’s go in and see Wyman,’ he suggested to the sheriff.

‘Okay,’ replied Bush. He unlocked the heavy iron door that shut off the cells from the office and they entered together. They found Tom Wyman sitting on a bunk, his chin cupped in his hand, staring out the barred window that opened on to the street.

‘Why didn’t yuh let ’em go on with it?’ he said morosely to Hatfield. ‘They’d have got it over in a hurry and that woulda been better’n waitin’.’

‘You snap outa it,’ Hatfield told him. ‘Your being here is a good thing—it’s liable to help a lot toward bustin’ up one of the most vicious gangs that ever operated along the Border. Now I want yuh to tell me straight just how yuh happened to be in that alley last night.’

Wyman stared at him, his eyes brightening with new hope.

‘Yuh don’t figger I did it, then?’ he asked.

‘No,’ Hatfield replied, ‘I don’t, and neither does the sheriff. Now get goin’ and answer my question.’

Wyman drew a deep breath and squared his shoulders.

'It was like this,' he said. 'Yesterday evenin' a feller come up to me on the street. I didn't know him, but he said he was a swamper at the Dust Layer and said Wade Hansford had sent him to hunt me up. He said Wade had been thinking about what happened between him and me in the Dust Layer day before yesterday and was feelin' bad about it. Figgered he hadn't done just the right thing. Said he wanted to see me and have a talk with me. Asked me to come inter the back room at nine o'clock. Said he would be workin' there and to come right in through the back door.'

'Didn't it strike yuh sorta funny for him to ask yuh to come in by way of the back door?' Hatfield asked.

'Nope,' Wyman replied, 'can't say as it did. Yuh see, I usta hang around in the Dust Layer considerable before—before I had my trouble last year. I knowed Wade's habits. Knowed he did all his book work in that back room and usta stay there till late at night. He usually locked the door inter the saloon so he wouldn't be disturbed. I allus figgered Wade for a squareshooter, too, and it didn't seem unnacherel that he'd get to feelin' it wasn't just the right thing to kick a man when he was down, and of co'hse I was willin' to meet him halfway. I was right up to the mouth of the alley a coupla minutes before nine o'clock when I heard a yell. It was dark in there and I stopped and listened a minute. Didn't hear anythin' more and moseyed on in. Stumbled over Hansford's body right outside the back door. Before I even got a chance to see who it was, the door opened and folks came boilin' out. Yuh know the rest.'

'Do yuh think Hansford really made that appointment for yuh to meet him at nine o'clock?' Hatfield asked. It was the sheriff who answered.

'I'd be willin' to swear he didn't,' said Bush. 'Yuh see, he had his meetin' with Bulkley at the bank for nine o'clock. It's just a coupla minutes walk to the bank by way of the alley. He wouldn't have been likely to make two meetin's for nine o'clock, would he?'

'Not apt to,' Hatfield agreed. He turned to Tom Wyman.

'You just sit tight and take it easy,' he told the young rancher. 'I know it isn't pleasant to be locked up, but right now it's the best thing for yuh. We'll just let folks go on thinkin' there's a tight case against yuh and mebbe that'll throw some smart jiggers off their guard.' He turned to the sheriff.

'Bush,' he said, 'I want yuh to give Wyman a gun to keep under his pillow.'

The sheriff stared. 'Well,' he said, 'if that ain't a plumb unusual thing to give a prisoner charged with murder!'

'Tom is a sorta unusual prisoner,' Hatfield returned, his white, even teeth suddenly flashing in a smile. 'And,' he added significantly, 'he might have use for it.'

The sheriff wagged his head in bewilderment. 'Hatfield,' he complained querulously, 'yuh don't happen to be one of these here hypnotizin' fellers I've heard about, do yuh? You make a man do things he never had no notion of doin'! Okay, I'll slip Wyman a hawg-leg. Hope he doesn't use it on me if he happens to get tired of stayin' here.'

'I don't think yuh'll need to worry,' Hatfield chuckled. He raised his head at the sound of a feminine voice in the outer office.

'Reckon that'll be Miss Teri,' he said. 'I figger Tom will be the better for a little talk with her.'

It *was* Teri Wright. When Hatfield and the sheriff returned to the outer room, leaving the cell door wide open behind them, Teri said nothing. Only she walked over to Jim Hatfield, stood on tiptoe, reached up and drew his face down within her reach and kissed him squarely on the mouth.

'I'd be willin' to stand a coupla mobs off for pay like that,' sighed old Moreman Miller. 'Oh, to be fifty or sixty agin!'

An hour later, Hatfield met Teri at the bank. The conference with old Banks Buster was satisfactory, Circle J owner being well pleased with the payment made on the Running W indebtedness. Teri rode back to the spread, but Hatfield had a number of chores to attend to in town.

One was a trip to the railroad telegraph office, where he found a message from Captain Bill McDowell awaiting him. It consisted of two terse sentences.

Suspected of murder and robbery in New Mexico (the message read). Nothing proved.

But the cryptic words seemed eminently satisfactory to the Lone Wolf, who left the office with thoughtful eyes and the concentration furrow deep between his black brows.

The lovely blue dusk was sifting down from the hills like smoky dust when Hatfield, his chores completed, repaired to the Dust Layer for a bite to eat. He found business going on as usual. The same barkeeps were behind the bar. Bart Cole, the yellow-haired dealer at the big poker table was handling the cards with smooth efficiency. But as he reached the end of the bar, Hatfield stood staring.

Hatless and coatless, moving about among the tables with an air of authority, was the big craggy-browed man with the scarred hand.

The bartender noted the direction of Hatfield's glance.

'That's the new boss,' he said with a jerk of his head. 'That's Si Releford. He bought the place from Pore Wade Hansford yesterday just a few hours before he was killed.'

## Chapter Nine

## RUSTLERS STRIKE

As Hatfield stood at the bar, sipping his drink, Silas Releford approached him.

'I just wanta say, feller,' Releford began with gruff cordiality, 'that I don't hold no hard feelin's over what happened here the night you and me had the run-in. That old feller riled me and I flew off the handle. I'm allus goin' off half-cocked, like to-day. Reckon it's just my way. Like that business of the jail to-day. I cottoned to Wade Hansford fust off and it hit me hard when he was done in. I was plumb het up. All I could think of was to get my hands on that murderin' sidewinder what did for him. You sorta brought me to my senses and I seed I was doin' plumb wrong. Let the law take its course. I reckon we can trust it to do the right thing. Hope yuh don't hold nothin' agin me.'

'What's happened is water under the bridge,' Hatfield replied noncommittally.

'Glad yuh feel that way about it,' Releford exclaimed heartily. 'Hope yuh'll keep on comin' in. We'll try and treat yuh right. Have one on the house.'

Tom Wyman had his hearing the following day and was bound over for action by the grand jury. The town had calmed down and there was no further talk of lynching, although the general consensus of opinion was that Wyman was guilty as hell. Si Releford appeared to run an orderly place and proved likely to become popular with the customers. Hatfield dropped in for a few minutes after Wyman's hearing.

A high stakes poker game was in progress at the big table presided over by Bart Cole. Men stood about in groups, silently watching the game. Hatfield unobtrusively joined them, standing almost directly behind the dealer, his great height enabling him to look over the shoulders of men in front of him. For some time he stood with his gaze passing directly over Cole's yellow head, apparently absorbed in the play. Then he strolled back to the bar and thoughtfully sipped his drink. Si Releford nodded cordially as he passed by, and motioned to the barkeep to refill Hatfield's glass.

'Going out of his way to be nice,' the Ranger mused as he accepted one on the house.

Business went on as usual at the Running W spread. Hatfield and his men were busy getting a second shipping herd together. In spare moments they occupied themselves with the construction of a new ranchhouse, although Teri declared she was perfectly comfortable in the tight little shack they had hurriedly thrown together for her occupancy.

'Yuh'll need more room when yuh get married,' Hatfield told her.

Teri said nothing, but her blue eyes were

misty.

'Don't be worrying,' Hatfield comforted her. 'Everything is going to work out all right.'

'Everybody firmly believes he's guilty,' Teri replied.

'Not everybody,' Hatfield countered. 'You don't believe so, and neither does the sheriff, and neither do I. That had ought to be enough.'

'But none of us will be on the jury,' Teri said gloomily.

'The case will never come before a jury,' Hatfield told her with quiet confidence.

Teri gave him a grateful look that was tinged with perplexity.

'You make me believe it when you say it that way, Jim,' she said, 'but I can't understand why. You are a strange man for a wandering cowboy.'

'Uh-huh,' Hatfield agreed, smiling slightly, 'for a wandering cowboy.'

In the meanwhile, Hatfield did a lot of riding through the grim Embrujada Hills to the south-west. He learned that Stiffy Jones was right when he maintained that it was practically impossible for a mounted man to negotiate them. They were a jumble of gorges, canyons, jagged rimrocks, cliffs and precipitous slopes. Canyon emptied from canyon and the jagged walls were honey-combed with caves and crevices. The utter confusion was intensified by the dense growth which choked the canyons and covered the slopes.

'But just the same, I'll bet my last peso those hellions have a hideout somewhere in here,' the Lone Wolf told his horse. 'They know how to get to it and cover their tracks. The gent who's running that sidewinder outfit sure knows this country—knows it as if he'd spent a long time in it, and that gives him a decided advantage over anybody who's new to the section. But he'll slip, feller, sooner or later they allus do. That is if he doesn't slip one over on us fust, and if he does, it's liable to be the last we'll ever know anything about. He's mean as a striped-back snake and smart as a tree full of owls.'

A week passed and another. Tom Wyman still languished in jail awaiting action by the grand jury which was due to meet the following month, but Sheriff Bush made his confinement as pleasant as possible and Teri Wright visited him frequently. Stiffy Jones, who firmly believed that Wyman was guilty, made a sententious remark.

'Yuh'll notice,' Stiffy said to Hatfield, 'that nobody's heard or seen hide or hair of the Death Riders since Wyman was locked up.'

'Mebbe they've reformed,' Hatfield replied.

'Cut off a snake's head, and the rest of the varmint don't give yuh no trouble,' Stiffy declared grimly.

But Stiffy's complacent optimism was due for a decided jar in the near future.

Old Banks Buster had gotten a great shipping herd together. Part of the beefs were from his own big spread, others had been purchased from neighbouring ranchers. Buster had hired hands to augment his already large force of riders, for he was taking no chances with his valuable herd.

'I won't feel easy till these cows are safe in the construction camp yard,' he told his foreman.

'Nobody is gonna be damn fool enough to tackle an outfit of this size,' declared the foreman. 'If they do, we'll make it so hot for them they'll think Hell is a coolin' off place when they get there.'

Buster figured it would require the best part of two days to make the drive to the construction camp with the big herd. He planned to camp somewhere in the neighbourhood of the Running W spread, about the half-way point along the trail to the construction camp. With this in mind, he took his chuck wagon along. He himself would drive the unwieldy wannigan.

The drive got under way and rolled south by west. Buster was complacent, even exultant, as from his high perch on the wagon seat he looked over the sea of shaggy backs and tossing horns and observed his alert riders trailing the herd along. He had started the drive at the first streak of dawn, being desirous of making the crossing at Mud River before the sun was slanting westward. It would be much easier to get the beefs into the water with the sun at their backs. Were it shining in their eyes, making it difficult for them to see the opposite bank, it would be almost impossible to get them to go into the water. The crossing where he aimed to start the swim was the only practical way across the river for a good twenty miles in either direction. Here the trail ran down a steep sag to the water's edge, and up a corresponding sag on the far side. Above and below were precipitous bluffs which a horseman could not negotiate, much less a herd of cows. The bluffs were not very high, but they were practically straight-up-and-down, their crests grown with thick and tall brush, their sides of crumbly shale and cracked stone. On either side they flanked the trail and the crossing with only the one narrow gut leading down to the water.

A quarter of a mile or so from the river, Buster's foreman rode back to the wagon rumbling along in the wake of the herd to consult with the boss.

'It's gonna be a big swimmin,' said the foreman, an anxious look in his eyes. 'That damn river is up. Must have been hard rains further nawth yesterday and last night.'

'We can make it,' Buster declared confidently. 'Head 'em straight across and don't let 'em double back. She ain't so wide, even if the water is a mite high. Shove 'em inter the swimmin' water, Hank, and keep 'em movin'. Glad I logged this damn wagon before we started. Had a notion we might need 'em.'

He glanced complacently at the long logs lashed on each side of the wagon and projecting beyond its ends. Those logs would serve to float the wagon and steady it. Buster was an expert teamster and expected no difficulty in getting the wagon across the swollen stream.

The herd streamed down the gut to the water's edge and the yelling cowboys sent them into the stream. In a moment the surface was speckled with heads, the air filled with the hollow clashing of horns. The cows bumped in tangled masses, bawled madly. But they streaked it like shooting stars across a yellow sky for the far side of the stream.

The leaders struck solid ground, floundered through the shallows, shaking the drops from their glistening hides in showers of silver rain, and went pounding up the far sag, sensing good grass atop the rise. After them poured the main body of the herd with the urging cowboys bringing up the rear. With the exception of a few point and swing riders on the down side of the stream, the entire outfit was in the rear, with the floating wagon and its swimming horses still farther behind. The only movement apparent was the herd streaming up the trail, the only sound, the noise of its passing. The growth crowned bluffs stretched north and south, devoid of sound or motion.

And then without warning, from the bristle of growth a little to the north of the crossing spurted lances of yellowish flame. The air rocked and quivered to the roar of gunfire. The point men nearest the shore whirled from their saddles and vanished beneath the yellow waters. A swing man, farther back, screamed shrilly and reeled, but kept his seat and managed to turn his maddened horse. The compact body of the outfit, bunched together behind the swimming herd, ducked and yelled as lead hissed over their heads. A chance shot struck the off-swinger—one of the two horses in the middle of the six-horse wagon team—wounded it fatally. The pain-crazed animal went under and came up snorting and plunging and lashing out with all four hoofs. To make matters worse it caught its foreleg in the crosstree of the leader ahead. In a moment the team was completely beyond control. The leaders swerved downstream, were thrown off their swimming stride. They doubled back, the front wheels swung around and locked and over went the wagon.

Old Banks Buster, with rare presence of mind, dived off upstream as the wagon careened and was saved from being caught in the welter and drowned. He grabbed hold of a stirrup strap as his riders came surging back across the stream to escape the hail of lead pouring from the growth atop the far bluff. He held on grimly until the swimming horse reached shallow water.

The remainder of the herd still in the water, maddened by the turmoil behind them, boiled across the river and tore, bawling and bellowing, up the far sag to stream over the crest.

The gunfire atop the bluff had abruptly ceased. As the last of the herd skalleyhooted over the crest, masked riders bulged out of the growth on either side and closed in on the herd, stampeding it westward across the level ground.

'After the blankety-blanks!' bawled old Banks Buster, dancing up and down with rage.

The Circle J riders urged their horses back into the water. They were half-way across the yellow river when the growth atop the bluff again blazed fire and smoke. Bullets spatted all around the riders and their swimming horses.

They tried to answer the fire, but the back of a swimming and frightened horse isn't a very good platform from which to shoot. And besides, there was nothing to be seen to shoot at. As the slugs came closer, they again turned their horses and retreated. Cursing viciously with their horses blowing and snorting, they scrambled back on solid ground once more. They waited a while, then again attempted the crossing, only to be driven back again.

A third time, after a much longer wait, they cautiously entered the water, rifles at the ready, eyes fixed on the silent crest of the bluff.

Half-way across—two-thirds—with their nerves strained to the breaking point, with the ominous bristle of growth silent and motionless.

'If they cut loose now, we're goners,' muttered a young puncher, shoving his rifle to the fore with a shaking hand.

They reached the bank unmolested and toiled up the sag. When they reached the crest, the herd was nowhere in sight. Only the dark loom of the hills to the west hinted at where it had vanished. Grimly they set out to trail the stolen cattle, but their horses were exhausted by the prolonged battle with the river and they could make but little speed. Nightfall caught them in the hills and it was impossible to follow the trail in the dark. Utterly worn out, discouraged, and bitter with anger, they turned back for the weary ride to Creston and the sheriff's office.

* * *

The Running W hands were aroused by the shouting of the Circle J outfit as they paused at the spread on their way to town. They tumbled out and got the news of the latest outrage.

Jim Hatfield immediately took charge of the situation.

'You fellers are all in,' he told the Circle J's. 'Flop in the bunkhouse and pound yore ears for a spell. I'll send a man to town to notify the sheriff. The rest of us will see what we can do.

'Get yore rigs on,' he directed his men. 'We're riding.'

Old Stiffy Jones growled querulously as they swept away from the spread.

'I don't see how yuh can figger to do anythin' in this pitch dark,' he complained. 'The moon's all hid by clouds and them hills are black as the inside of a bull in fly time.'

'Playing a hunch,' Hatfield told him. 'Mebbe there's nothing to it, but then again mebbe it'll work out.'

Stiffy snorted with disgust and subsided to pessimistic mutterings.

They rode south-west through the night until they reached the black mouth of White Horse Canyon. Hatfield turned into the rock-walled gorge. Dawn was already streaking the sky and before long it was light enough to distinguish objects even in the depths of the canyon. Their progress was necessarily slow, but Hatfield seemed in no particular hurry. As the light strengthened he even checked the pace.

Above, the slit of sky that pressed down upon the towering walls became a tender blue, then flamed golden. Finally a sword of light burned to the zenith. It fell downward, pierced the gloom of the canyon floor and outlined the trail they were following.

Hatfield pulled up and dismounted.

Wordless he pointed to the surface of the trail. It was deeply scarred by fresh hoofprints.

'By gum! Yuh hit it right!' old Stiffy exploded. 'A big herd has passed along here and not many hours back.'

'That's how I figger it,' Hatfield replied quietly. 'Okay, let's get going. Take it easy now, and keep yore eyes skun and yore ears open.'

Tensely alert, they followed the trail of hoofs. They reached the mouth of the narrow side canyon that opened into White Horse. The brush-choked mouth showed evidence of the recent passage of horses and cattle.

'They turned in there as I figgered they would,' Hatfield explained. 'It was them, all right. This tough brush springs back into place and the bent branches straighten out mighty fast. The shape it is in now shows a herd passed through only a few hours back. I figger this is their short-cut to the desert and on to the River. Let's go, but don't take any chances. We're up against a salty outfit that doesn't miss any bets.'

They passed into the canyon. Soon they reached the burned-over area where they had so narrowly escaped destruction. They coughed and sneezed in the clouds of ash churned up by the horses' irons, but were encouraged by the prints of cattle still trending down-canyon.

Finally they reached a long stretch of stony,

barren ground where the fire had burned itself out. No trace of the passing herd showed on the iron-hard soil, but the towering rock walls on either side guaranteed that the herd could not have turned.

Another mile, and they paused on the bank of a sizeable swift, shallow stream that poured from a narrow slit in the east wall of the canyon, flowed straight across it and dived into a like crevice in the west wall. So narrow was the crevice that the hurrying water washed the rock wall on either side, with no intermediate stretch of beach.

They waded their horses across the stream, the icy water of which was not quite belly-deep, and continued down the canyon. The soil was still hard and stony, but on a softer patch, Hatfield's keen eyes noted a few scattered hoof-marks.

'Could those hellions have doubled back to White Horse Canyon?' he wondered.

Another hour of riding and they reached the canyon mouth. Before them stretched the wide expanse of the desert, its sands gleaming golden in the morning sunlight, chimney rocks, spires and buttes starting up starkly from the flat surface, cactuses brandishing weirdly deformed arms. Arid, profitless, devoid of life or motion save for the hot shimmer of the air above its glaring surface, it stretched onward to the distant Rio Grande.

Just beyond the canyon mouth were a few

hoofmarks; but a wind had been rising for some time and the sands were shifting, whispering eerily to themselves as the grains moved one upon another.

Hatfield eyed the desert with a darkening face. He shook his head in weary disgust.

'That infernal wind!' he growled. 'It's filled the tracks!' His men stared gloomily southward.

'The hellions might have turned any direction,' grunted Stiffy. 'It was a good hunch, Jim, but the luck went wrong. If that damn wind hadn't started blowing, I've a notion we coulda tracked 'em right to the River and caught 'em before they coulda got across. It's a bad crossin' down there. As it is, it's like huntin' for a pertickler tick in a flock of sheep.'

Hatfield was forced to agree. Reluctantly he gave the order to turn back.

## Chapter Ten

## OUT-SMARTED

Creston seethed over the latest depredation of the Death Riders. Sheriff Bush and his posse combed the hills with barren results. Men who had been saying that the arrest of Tom Wyman would put an end to the activities of the sinister band looked at one another askance.

Jim Hatfield smiled grimly and said nothing.

Hatfield was, in fact, about ready for a final and unexpected move, but he hesitated to act.

'Old Stiffy is sorta wrong,' he mused. 'It isn't enough to smash the snake's head if the body is still wiggling around and maybe all set to grow a new head. There are brains in that outfit and I've a notion they mightn't all be in *one* head.'

And then events played into his hands, although for a time they appeared to be anything but to his advantage.

Hatfield had spent a busy day in town attending to sundry chores for the spread, one of which included a worrying interview with old Banks Buster who had been hard hit by the loss of his big herd and was desperately in need of money. With much to think about, just as dusk was falling, he dropped into the Dust Layer for a bite to eat before riding back to the spread.

Si Releford, as usual, greeted him with boisterous heartiness.

'Just got some new stuff in to-day for my puhsonal use,' said Releford. 'I want yuh to have a snort of it with me.'

He bustled behind the bar, procured a bottle and held it up with a triumphant grin.

'Yuh don't come by this often,' he said. He carefully chose two clean glasses from the back bar, filled them to the brim and shoved one to Hatfield. Raising his own, he downed the contents at a gulp, smacking his lips with appreciation. Hatfield sipped his judiciously.

'Does taste sorta different,' he admitted.

'It *is* different,' declared Releford, refilling the glasses. He drank his own off and passed from behind the bar.

'Got a little business to 'tend to,' he said. 'Take yore time, feller, I'll be seein' yuh.'

Hatfield discussed his drink slowly. It seemed to him that the flavour of the liquor was somewhat superior to the first glass.

'The other was too close to the cork, chances are,' he decided.

He had had a hard day and he began to feel very weary, unusually so, in fact. As he gazed at the whirling figures on the dance floor they seemed to blur before his eyes. Once he caught himself nodding. He set the empty glass down heavily and leaned on the bar, growing more tired by the minute. His hunger had left him and his greatest desire was for sleep. Abruptly he decided to leave without eating.

'If I make it to the spread without falling outa the hull I'll be lucky,' he muttered as he dragged his heavy feet to the door.

The trip across the street to the hitchrack where Goldy was tied seemed amazingly long. He fumbled the tether loose with uncertain fingers and mounted sluggishly. He slumped in the saddle as he rode out of town and it was all he could do to keep his eyes from closing. He was perhaps half a mile out of town and half asleep in the saddle, when he dully sensed a beat of fast hoofs behind him. He wondered idly who it could be, but it seemed too much of an effort to turn around and see. He realized that his chin was resting on his breast and that he was swaying in the hull. He jerked himself erect with an effort, shook his head to clear it of cobwebs. The speeding hoofs were close now and he forced himself to turn round. But his eyelids were drooping and he couldn't seem to summon enough strength to raise them.

The hoofbeats clattered up on either side of him. Another instant and rough hands were layed on him. He tried to struggle, to reach for his guns, but his muscles seemed to turn to water, his movements slow and clumsy. Then came a crashing blow on the head and the world dissolved in rushing blackness. He slumped forward until his face was buried in the horse's coarse mane.

Long afterward, it seemed to him, Hatfield recovered sufficiently to realize that his horse was splashing through water, but as he attempted to raise his aching head, a deadly nausea rushed over him and he sank back into unconsciousness.

When he completely regained his senses, he discovered he was lying on a rough bunk. He attempted to move his hands and could not. His wrists were firmly bound together in front of him. A tentative tug at his ankles assured him that they were likewise secured. His mind was still hazy, but clearing rapidly. He began recalling and analyzing recent past events.

'Drugged!' was his conclusion. 'That big hellion slipped a doze in my drink. I thought that first glass tasted sorta funny. He was smart, though, used something with very little flavour to it, and washed my mouth out quick with a second drink. Well, I've tangled my twine for sure this time. Had oughta been on the look-out for something like that. A smart outfit, all right, and they sure put one over!'

He became aware of voices close by. Slanting his half-closed eyes sideways, he took in the surroundings. He was in what was evidently a rather large one-roomed cabin built stoutly of logs chinked with clay and ceiled with heavy boards. Directly above the bunk on which he lay was a small window barred with iron. Across the room was a closed door and back of the door his own cartridge belts and holstered guns hung from a peg. On one side was an iron cooking-stove that glowed redly through its grates. There was rough crockery and a few cooking utensils on shelves or suspended from pegs. Several rifles stood in a corner. Built against the fourth wall was a second bunk with tumbled blankets. Underneath it lay a couple of saddles and a pair of old boots.

In the middle of the room was a crudely built table and seated at it discussing a meal were two men. Their faces were vaguely familiar, and in a moment Hatfield recognized them as two of the group that had accompanied Silas Releford the night he had the run-in with old Stiffy.

The men were talking as they ate. Hatfield lay motionless with closed eyes and listened.

'I don't see why we can't just knock that hellion on the head and get it over with,' one remarked in querulous tones, darting a glance at the motionless Ranger.

'Yuh know what the boss's orders are,' the other replied. 'He has use for that jigger. He's the bait to get that fool gal here with. She's plumb loco about him and she'll come askalleyhootin' when she gets word that's supposed to come from him.'

'What in blazes does the boss want with her, anyhow?' the first speaker demanded.

The other shrugged his heavy shoulders. 'I don't ask the boss no questions—it ain't healthy,' he grunted. 'Yuh'll find out, when yuh get to know him better, that he's got a good reason for everythin' he does. Well, if yuh're finished eatin' we'll get ready to ride. Got a long trip ahead of us. We round up the boys and have them back here right after dark tonight.'

'Will the boss be here then?'

'Nope. He won't get in until nigh t'morrer mawnin'. To-day's payday, and it would look funny for him to pull out early with business boomin' like it will be.'

'I thought to-morrer was payday?'

'Hell, it's after midnight, ain't it. That makes payday to-day. Let's get goin'. I'll look over that hellion fust, though.'

Chairs scraped back from the table. Hatfield heard one of the men approach the bunk. Hands tugged at his bonds, found them secure.

'Still out like a horned toad in cold weather,' the man muttered. 'Them knock-out drops the boss uses is lightnin'!'

For a few minutes more Hatfield, lying motionless and breathing heavily in simulated unconsciousness, heard the men moving about the room. Then there was the sound of an opening and closing door. A key grated in a lock. Footsteps died away. There was a period of silence, broken finally by a click of horses' irons passing the cabin and then ceasing abruptly. The silence descended again, and remained unbroken save for, muffled by distance and the thick walls of the cabin, the occasional bawling of a steer.

For a long time Jim Hatfield lay quietly on the bunk, listening intently. He was puzzled by that sudden cessation of hoofbeats which seemed to indicate that the two owlhoots had pulled up a little distance from the cabin. Gradually he became conscious of a faint murmuring that blunted the sharp edge of the silence. Finally he catalogued it as the ripple of running water not far off. A sudden explanation of the abrupt ending of the hoofbeats came to him.

'The hellions rode into the water,' he muttered. 'Must be a crick they needed to cross running close by.'

Assured that the outlaws had really departed, he began to tug at the cords that bound his wrists. Soon, however, he was convinced that he was powerless to loosen them. His eyes roved over the room in search of something to assist his efforts.

Only the red glow from the stove grates lighted the room, barely enough for him to distinguish objects. His glance fixed on the table. Dirty dishes rested upon it. He writhed his body to the edge of the bunk until he lost his balance and fell.

He struck the floor with a jar that set every joint to creaking. For a moment he lay half-stunned. Then he rolled and twisted until he was within reach of the table. Raising his bound feet he thrust at it with all his strength.

Over went the table, to the accompaniment of a prodigious clatter of breaking dishes. With a grunt of satisfaction, Hatfield continued to roll and writhe until he was in the midst of the shattered crockery. He got his bound wrists over a fragment and sawed the cords that secured them against a sharp edge.

But the fragment slipped and slid and he could get no firm purchase against it. After an eternity of effort, in the course of which the stout cord was barely frayed, he gave it up with a disgusted oath. Panting from the exertion, he lay still and considered the situation.

That he was in a very tight spot he very well knew. He suffered no delusion as to what would be his fate when the 'boss' the two owlhoots had mentioned arrived on the scene and he, Hatfield, had fulfilled his purpose, that of luring the 'gal' to the cabin.

The girl in question, Hatfield was satisfied, was none other than Teri Wright.

'The hellion is figgering on pulling out,' he muttered to himself. 'He's decided the section is getting too hot and with the hauls he's made he feels it's a good time to move on. Chances are he's got one more big job lined up. One thing is sure for certain, he isn't going to leave anybody behind who knows anything. If I am still here when he gets here—well!'

He eyed the rifles in the corner, wondering if they were loaded, and if there was a chance to shoot the cords loose from his wrists, but dismissed the expedient as unfeasible. His glance roamed about the darkening room in search of some cutting edge against which to rub the cords, and found none. Finally his gaze centred on the dully glowing grates of the stove. The fire was dying down and soon it would be pitch dark in the closed cabin.

Suddenly his eyes glowed with inspiration. He had a chance after all, a desperate chance—a gamble against horrible death, but—a chance.

'Mebbe I'll just get myself roasted alive, but it's wuth trying—I haven't anything to lose, anyhow,' he muttered as he writhed towards the squat stove.

Getting into position, he doubled up his legs and kicked out with all his strength.

Over went the stove under the terrific impact. Its lids rolled off, its doors flew open. Glowing coals cascaded out and bounced all over the room. Almost instantly there was a smell of burning.

Hatfield flopped and twisted frantically to where a red mass lay on the floor, its edges already greying under the light of a flicker of flame rising from the dry and greasy floorboards. He levered his wrists up until the cords were resting on the coals. Sweat popped out on his face as the heat seared his wrists, but he set his teeth and pressed the cords against the red embers.

All about him now were flickering flames where the coals were eating into the floor boards. Smoke began to thicken. The air grew hot and stifling.

The blankets on the bunk were smouldering. Suddenly they flared into flame under the draft fanning through the barred window. The wooden bunk began to snap and crackle. Smoke billowed up, acrid, choking smoke. Hatfield coughed and gagged. He could feel the cords charring, but the process was unbearably slow. He strained at his pain-seared wrists with all his strength, but the stubborn ropes resisted his efforts. A glance upward showed him that the ceiling boards had caught from the flames pouring up the wall from the burning bunk. Other flames were crawling along the floor, growing larger by the second. The air was almost unbreathable with smoke and heat.

Again Hatfield strained at the cords. They loosened a trifle. He relaxed his muscles, put forth a mighty effort.

The weakened cords snapped, fell away. Hatfield writhed to a sitting position and with numbed hands fumbled at the knots that secured his ankles. After what seemed an eternity of futile effort he loosened them and staggered to his feet, his legs wooden from retarded circulation. He lurched across the blazing room to the peg from which his guns were suspended, secured them and buckled them on. Then he rushed to the door and hurled his weight against it. It creaked and groaned but resisted his efforts.

Staggering back, he plucked up the heavy table and dashed it against the barrier. The planks splintered, but held.

Again and again he hurled the unwieldy obstacle against the door and still it stubbornly resisted. His head was whirling, hot flashes were storming before his eyes. His throat seemed closing. He coughed and choked in the heat.

Dropping the table, he drew a gun. With fumbling fingers he located where the lock should be. With the gun muzzled as close against it as he dared, he fired shot after shot.

At the fourth shot there was a jangle of parting metal. Hatfield again hurled his weight against the door. It flew wide open and he stumbled through, breathing in great gulps of cool, fresh air.

As soon as he got the smoke out of his eyes, Hatfield saw by the light of the burning cabin a sight that gladdened his heart.

Tethered under a rough leanto not far from the cabin was Goldy, his big sorrel. His riding gear lay heaped in a corner.

Almost at his feet was a swift stream that reflected the light of the blazing cabin. It flowed from a cleft in a wall of stone against which the cabin was built.

A full moon shone in the sky and Hatfield could see that the cabin sat at the end of an almost circular valley, or amphitheatre, walled about by towering cliffs that soared up to jagged rimrock broken by crags and spires. The floor of the bowl was thickly grown with brush and trees, but in open spaces he could see cattle grazing on the sparse grass.

'The Death Riders' hangout,' he muttered. 'A hidden valley in the hills with just one mighty narrow door.'

When he had caught his breath, he got the rig on Goldy and with a last glance at the cabin, which was being swiftly reduced to a heap of ashes, he sent the sorrel into the stream and into the black cleft from which it flowed. For a mile or more he splashed between closely encroaching rock walls. Then the cleft opened into a narrow canyon.

The stream, as Hatfield suspected, proved to be the same that cut across the scorched gorge which opened from White Horse Canyon.

'No wonder we lost track of Banks Buster's herd when we tried to trail it,' he muttered. 'The hellions drove it into the stream, turned it inter the cleft and snaked it along until they had it safe in their hole-in-the-wall hideout. That's where they figgered to hold it, along with the other cows they been widelooping, until they're ready to slide it out and drive it across the river to a good market. A plumb smart outfit, all right, but I've a notion it's about trail's end for the sidewinders.'

He quickened Goldy's pace and rode swiftly back along the way he had traversed with his Running W hands but a few days before.

Dawn was streaking the sky when Hatfield reached the Running W. Without hesitation, he aroused Teri Wright, who stared wide-eyed at the blackened, dishevelled face and form.

'I want yuh to ride to town, pronto,' he told her, forestalling the questions that began pouring from her lips. 'Go to the jail, just as if yuh were paying Tom Wyman a visit. Get word to the sheriff. Tell him and Trout Mason to hustle out here. Tell them to ride north outa town and circle through the hills. And tell him to bring plenty of handcuffs with him. You stay in town to-night and keep outa sight. Don't come back to the spread until yuh hear from me. Understand?'

'No, I don't,' Teri replied, 'but I'll do whatever you say.'

The sheriff and his chief deputy arrived at the spread shortly before noon, bursting with questions which Hatfield cut short.

'I want yuh to appoint the whole Running W outfit special deputies,' he told Bush. 'We got a chore to do.'

In a few terse sentences he outlined the happenings of the night before. The sheriff swore exultantly.

'We'll get 'em!' he exclaimed. 'We'll bag the hull bunch. But who's the boss they talked about?'

'You'll see, when the time comes,' Hatfield told him grimly. 'We'll ride as soon as we eat.'

A hasty meal was grabbed. Then the Running W hands, having been sworn in as special deputies, saddled up and rode in the wake of Jim Hatfield and the sheriff.

Hatfield circled through the hills to the west and then led his posse into White Horse Canyon. Through the fire-scorched gorge and the narrow, water-choked cleft they made their way. They approached the hidden valley with caution but found it deserted. The cabin had burned to a heap of ashes and charred timbers.

'A plumb perfect hole-in-the-wall,' said the sheriff, glancing down the great bowl and up at the jagged rimrock which flamed with the fires of sunset. 'Nobody would ever think of climbing up them crags to see what was behind 'em, and if they did, they wouldn't see anythin' down here but trees and brush.'

'Yes, a dozen herds of cows could be hid here and kept outa sight as long as necessary,' Hatfield agreed. 'I figger yuh can count on finding the herd stole from Banks Buster, and the one that was widelooped the night the Running W ranchhouse was burned, and all the other beefs that have been rustled in this section of late. The hellions would figger to hold them until the fall roundup season when they could slip them across the river and get top prices for them. Chances are they'd lay low for a while before roundup time and let the section cool down. Then nobody would be on the look-out for wet cows, pertickler as all the spreads would be busy then with roundup work. A smart outfit, all right, and vicious as so many broken-backed rattlers.'

'They'll be broken-necked when we get through with them,' the sheriff promised.

As the light faded, they made their preparations, holed up in the brush out of sight and waited.

The wait was long and tiresome. It was fully

dark and the eastern crags were aglow with the silvery light of the rising moon behind them when the sound of horses splashing in the stream was heard. A little later shadowy figures loomed in the pale reflected light of the moonshine flowing up the sky.

Suddenly there was a chorus of exclamations. The owlhoots had noted the ruins of the burned cabin. They clumped together, peering and muttering. They were bunched thus in a bewildered mob when with a crackling roar a huge heap of oil-drenched brush flamed high, making the scene as light as day.

'Reach for the sky!' thundered Sheriff Bush. 'Yuh're kivered, yuh sidewinders!'

There was an instant of paralyzed silence. Then with a yell of terror, one of the outlaws went for his gun.

Jim Hatfield shot him before he could clear leather. The guns of the posse roared and three more owlhoots went down. The remainder, a half dozen villainous-looking characters, threw up their hands and yelled for mercy.

With the guns of his possemen trained upon them, Sheriff Bush passed behind the group, securing their hardware and snapping on handcuffs.

'Now what?' he asked Hatfield when the last of the Death Riders was securely ironed.

Hatfield turned to the Running W cowboys.

'You jiggers take charge of this bunch and bring 'em in to town,' he directed. 'Don't take any chances with them. Shoot to kill if they try to make a break. Sheriff, you and Mason come with me. We're gonna do some fast riding.'

## CHAPTER ELEVEN

## SHOWDOWN

In Creston the payday celebration had about roared itself out. Lights were being dimmed. The saloons and dance-halls were emptying as tired men sought sleep. Here and there a group of belated revellers shouted and sang. Little knots of hilarious cowboys skalleyhooted out of town, banging holes in the sky and whooping with the exuberance of alcohol and youthful spirits.

There were still quite a few late drinkers and gamesters in the big Dust Layer. Si Releford stood at the end of the bar checking the contents of the till. Weary bartenders polished glasses. The orchestra played a last listless number. Bart Cole sat back of the big poker table and shuffled the cards for a final hand. He glanced expectantly at Releford, who nodded his head slightly as he closed the till.

Abruptly the swinging doors flew back and a tall figure stepped into the room.

Jim Hatfield's stern face was bleak as chiselled granite, his eyes coldly grey as frozen water. Flanking him on either side were Sheriff Mack Bush and deputy Trout Mason, tense and watchful.

On Hatfield's broad breast gleamed *a silver star set on a silver circle*, the feared and honoured and respected badge of the Texas Rangers.

The groups in the saloon stood wide-eyed and hushed.

'Good gosh!' a voice suddenly exclaimed. 'That feller's a Texas Ranger!'

'Yeah!' whooped old Trout Mason, wild with excitement, 'I spotted him fust off—a Texas Ranger, and—*the Lone Wolf!*'

A stunned silence fell over the saloon. Men stared in awe at the almost legendary figure whose exploits were a byword for daring and achievement the length and breadth of Texas. *The Lone Wolf!*

Heedless of the sensation Mason's shout had produced, Jim Hatfield strode straight for the table behind which sat Bart Cole, his face livid, his eyes glaring. Hatfield's voice rang out, edged with steel:

'In the name of the State of Texas, I arrest you, *Burns Wright*, for the robbery and murder of Wade Hansford. Anything you may say—'

At the sound of that name on the Ranger's lips, the dealer surged erect. His right hand shot out like the head of a striking snake, his stubby little sleeve gun spatted against his palm.

But even as he pulled trigger he reeled back and fell with a crash, taking chair and table with him, his breast smashed and riddled by the slugs from Hatfield's Colt.

Apparently without taking aim, Hatfield fired across his right arm with his left-hand gun. Si Releford yelled with agony, spun around and pitched headlong to lie writhing and moaning, the gun he had drawn lying beside him on the floor.

Hatfield glanced quickly around the room, decided there was nothing to be feared from the stunned and cowering occupants. He holstered his guns, walked over and gazed down at the dead face of the man who had been known as Bart Cole, head dealer in the Dust Layer. He cast a glance at the moaning Releford.

'Prop him up and send for the doctor,' he directed. 'A smashed shoulder is all he's got. He's a weak sister and will talk to save his own hide. He can fill up the cracks if there are any that need filling. Might be one or two of the gang still running loose that he can give yuh a line on, Sheriff.'

Sheriff Bush came over and stood beside Hatfield.

'Jim,' he protested, jerking his thumb towards the dead dealer, 'that feller can't be Burns Wright. I rec'lect Wright well. He had black whiskers and coal-black hair. This feller ain't got no whiskers and his hair is yaller.'

Hatfield smiled slightly.

'Whiskers can be shaved off,' he answered, 'and bend down, Sheriff, and take a good look at the roots of his hair.'

Sheriff Bush obeyed.

'Why,' he exclaimed in bewildered tones, 'it's black down at the roots.'

'That's right,' Hatfield replied. 'They usually dye their hair when they want to disguise themselves, but Burns Wright worked in reverse. He bleached his.'

'But it *can't* be Burns Wright,' the sheriff insisted stubbornly. 'I saw Burns Wright buried, or his bones buried, anyhow.'

Hatfield smiled again, and shook his head.

'Nope, yuh didn't see Burns Wright buried, his bones neither,' he differed. 'What yuh saw buried were the bones of pore old Wun-Wun, the Chinese cook who usta work for the Running W. Burns Wright wasn't in the Running W ranchhouse when it was set afire.'

'And Wun-Wun was, and got burned up?'

'Nope. Just his dead body got burned up. Wun-Wun was murdered and his body placed downstairs in the ranchhouse so that bones would be found which folks would nacherly think belonged to Burns Wright. Wright and his Death Riders murdered Wun-Wun and Wright gave out that Wun-Wun had quit and gone away.'

‘Say,’ exclaimed the Sheriff, ‘let’s set down and have a drink! I’m gettin’ all mixed up. Straighten this mess out, will yuh, Hatfield? Who was the Boss of the Death Riders? Si Releford?’

‘Nope,’ Hatfield replied as they took chairs at a nearby table, ‘Releford was just a hired hand. Burns Wright was the head of the Death Riders, here and over in New Mexico where they operated under a different name.

‘Here comes Doc Beard and a coupla deputies,’ he remarked, glancing up. ‘I’ll want him to corroborate something I’ll have to say. Mason, while Doc’s patching up Releford, suppose you run over to the jail and get Tom Wyman. He’ll be released to-morrow anyhow, as soon as Judge Arbaugh convenes co’ht. The Rangers will go bail for him to-night. And yuh’ll need all the room yuh’ve got to accommodate the Death Riders when the boys get in with them.’

‘Chances are yuh’ll find him and old Moreman Miller settin’ up in the office playin’ cribbage,’ Sheriff Bush said. ‘Moreman’s heart will be plumb busted in two when Tom checks out. He says Wyman is the only cribbage player he ever met who could give him a good game.’

‘And while yuh’re at it, stop at the hotel and rouse up Miss Teri,’ Hatfield added. ‘I imagine she’s sitting up waiting to hear what’s happened.’

By the time the blaspheming Releford’s

wound was dressed and he was carted off to jail by the deputies, Mason arrived with Wyman and Teri Wright. Teri was bewildered, but starry-eyed. Wyman, as was not unnatural, looked decidedly relieved. When all were seated at the table, Hatfield resumed his story.

'Now how did yuh know it was Wun-Wun and not Wright who got burned up in the fire?' the sheriff asked.

Hatfield smiled. 'By the skull I found in the ruins after the fire burned down,' he said. 'It was pretty badly charred, but not enough to make identification impossible. I didn't think so much about it right at fust, for there was a chance, of co'hse, that Wright had left the ranchhouse before the fire without Stiffy or the other boys, Hank and Billy, knowing about it, and at that time I had no reason for suspecting Wright of anything. But when Wright didn't show up later, I got to thinking hard about it. I recalled something else, too. When I made it to Wright's bedroom from the attic I found the door to the lower floor shut tight. Of co'hse, a man *might* take time to close the door after him when he was running for his life to escape being burned alive, but it would be an unusual thing for him to do.'

'Couldn't the wind have blown the door shut?' the sheriff asked.

Hatfield shook his head. 'The door opened to the inside of the room,' he explained. 'With the fire burning downstairs, there would be a fierce draught pulling up the stairs, which would tend to keep the door open, not close it. Mighty soon, after Wright didn't show up, I was sure that he hadn't been in that room when the fire started. Wun-Wun would hardly have been there, either. A cook doesn't hang around in the boss's room late at night. So Wun-Wun must have been downstairs when the fire started, and it was logical to believe he wasn't alive when the fire started, otherwise he woulda walked out.

'But Stiffy told me Wun-Wun had left the spread two days before. Stiffy and the other boys saw him ride away, heading for New Mexico. So why would he be back in the ranchhouse if he hadn't been brought back, and the chances were if he was brought back, he was brought back dead.'

'But how did yuh know the skull yuh found didn't belong to Wright?' the sheriff asked.

Hatfield glanced at Doc Beard.

'Because,' he replied, 'I know the skull was not the skull of a Caucasian, as Wright undoubtedly was. There is a decided difference between the skull of a Caucasian and that of a Chinese. Only a limited knowledge of comparative anatomy is necessary to recognize that difference.'

'That's right,' put in Doc Beard. 'I can conclusively prove by measurements, if the skull in that grave is the skull of a Chinese.'

'Then a little later I had corroborative evidence,' Hatfield resumed. He drew from his pocket a little silver rod with a knob at one end.

'Know what it is?' he asked, laying it on the table.

'Why,' exclaimed Teri Wright, 'it's a chopstick. I've seen Chinese use them in California.'

'Exactly,' Hatfield agreed. 'It's the little dofunny a Chinaman uses to eat with instead of a fork. I took this one out of the pocket of one of the Death Riders who tried to rob the express car of the C & P flyer. He must have stolen it off pore old Wun-Wun after he was killed. Yuh see, the thing was tieing up. I was sure that Wun-Wun's body was in the ranchhouse when it burned and that the Death Riders had killed him. I was about sure by now, too, that Burns Wright was mixed up with the Death Riders, so I began working on that angle.'

He paused to roll a cigarette, smiling the while at his rapt listeners.

'I examined the masks worn by the Death Riders,' he continued. 'The paint on them was interesting. It was luminous paint that shone in the dark, making the skull pattern stand out. Now luminous paint isn't something yuh can buy in the average cow town. Yuh hafta send away for it, and folks in sections like this usually send to one of the big mail order houses when they want something they can't get at home. So I had Captain McDowell get busy on that angle. He learned that a shipment of luminous paint had been mailed to Burns Wright of the Running W. That's where Wright slipped bad. He had worked out a mighty cute scheme, but, as owlhoots usually do he'd slipped up on some little things. Like the closed door of his room, for instance. And like the safe I uncovered in the ruins of the Running W ranchhouse. The combination knob and the tumblers were intact, which showed that the safe had either been left unlocked or had been opened by working the combination and not smashed or blown open as one would expect to find it under the circumstances. And letting one of his side-winders go through Wun-Wun's pockets after he was killed. That cinched the case against Wright.'

'But why did he do it?' asked Teri. 'Why did he pretend to be burned up in the ranchhouse?'

'Because,' Hatfield replied quietly, 'he knew that sooner or later his past would catch up with him. He raised plenty of hell over in New Mexico. He claimed to have been in Arizona, but my experience has been that owlhoots usually claim to have come from some place not far from where they really were. Wright operated with a gang in New Mexico, but the law never managed to catch up with him although he was suspected of complicity in robbery and murder. New Mexico was getting too hot for him, though, so he moved his outfit over here and set up business in Texas. He managed to do away with Teri's father and take charge of the Running W, and that gave him a chance for a big killing. So he sold that big herd to Banks Buster and then had his men wideloop it. He got away with the herd and the twenty thousand dollars Buster paid for it as well. And he arranged so that it would appear he died in the ranchhouse fire, so nacherly suspicion would never be directed towards Burns Wright. There was another reason why he wanted to disappear as Burns Wright. That reason was Tom Wyman. He was worried about Wyman after he got out of the penitentiary. He'd figgered, when he framed Wyman, that he could be sent away for a long time. Wyman coming back in less than a year complicated things for him.'

'But why did he want to get Tom in trouble?' Teri wondered.

Hatfield smiled, his gaze resting on the blue-eyed girl.

'Because,' he said slowly, 'because Tom was young.'

'Because he was young!'

'Yes, Burns Wright happened to be a man who was born twenty years too soon. Remember, Teri, he was no blood relation of yores. He was just the adopted son of yore grandfather. He hardly knew you, and when he came back from New Mexico and took up with yore dad, the little girl he hardly remembered had grown up into a very attractive young lady. He tangled his twine over you, and when Tom Wyman came around and he saw Tom had the inside track he plumb hated Tom. So he got Tom framed inter that penitentiary, but when Tom came back a lot sooner than he expected the whole thing started over again. So he proceeded to frame Tom again and frame him proper.'

'And he came mighty nigh gettin' away with it, too,' muttered Wyman. 'How'd yuh figger Bart Cole was Burns Wright?'

'Well, when I decided that Burns Wright was not dead but just pretending to be, I also decided that he would hang around the section and would be cleverly disguised. I began looking out for a jigger who was just the opposite to what Burns Wright had been. Wright wore whiskers and had black hair, so I looked for a clean-shaven jigger with different coloured hair. Then Bart Cole happened along and took the job of head dealer at the Dust Layer. Right there I had something to go on. Wade Hansford had mentioned that Wright was a fust-class card dealer, so good in fact that he once jokingly offered him a job in the Dust Layer. Wright remembered that, so when he needed an excuse to stick around the section in disguise he murdered Pete Spencer, the head dealer, and got the job. Remember, Mason, that I mentioned the look of surprise frozen on Spencer's dead face. Spencer disappeared the day before the ranchhouse fire. He knew Wright well, of co'hse, and when he found Wright in his room he was surprised, not scared. He never had a chance any more than pore Hansford had. Hansford was killed by a knife in the back too, remember. That was another angle that tied up.

'When Captain McDowell tried to get a line on Wright, as Wright, in New Mexico or Arizona, there was nothing to be learned about a man answering his description, but when I sent along Bart Cole's description, it was different. I'd already decided that Cole was a jigger who had shaved off whiskers plumb recent.'

'How was that?' asked Sheriff Bush.

'Cole's cheeks and chin were pale, but there was suntan around his eyes and on the tops of his cheek bones,' Hatfield replied.

The sheriff shook his head in wordless admiration.

'The scar on his face helped his disguise, too,' Hatfield continued. 'Nobody around here knew he had that scar—the whiskers covered it. Chances are that was why he wore 'em. It was a badly healed knife cut and didn't help his looks anyway. I was getting mighty interested in Bart Cole, so I waited a while and then managed to get a good look at his hair. Right there he neglected another little thing. He didn't keep on bleaching his hair regularly, and down at the roots the black colour began to show as his hair grew out. That just about cinched the case. The name he was carrying helped, too.'

'How's that?'

Hatfield smiled, and rolled another cigarette before replying.

'It's been my experience,' he said, 'that when owlhoots take on a false name, they almost invariably choose one that is something like their real one. Teri told me that Burns Wright's real name was Burns Colver. Get the tie-up—Burns Colver—Bart Cole.

'Then along came Si Releford and bought the Dust Layer from Hansford for twenty thousand dollars, the exact amount the Death Riders lifted from the Running W safe. Mebbe just coincidence, but looked funny.

'I'd already spotted Releford as a member of the Death Riders because of that skull mask he lost that I picked up the night he had the run-in with old Stiffy. Wade Hansford was cashed in for the money he was carrying—the money Releford had paid for the saloon, and Tom Wyman was lured to the scene of the killing just at the right time to make it look almighty bad for him. Burns Wright's hand again.

'By that time I was sure Bart Cole was Burns Wright, but as yet I didn't know how to drop a loop on the Death Riders. I was getting nervous, too, for I figgered they were due to pull something else any day. But they were getting nervous about me. They didn't know for sure who or what I was. Chances were they figgered I was another owlhoot trying to horn in on their game, but I'd already caused them plenty of trouble and they figgered it was time to get rid of me. So Releford put a smart one over on me with that doped drink. I reckon if I hadn't got the breaks there, things mighta worked out different.'

'*You* might call it "the breaks," but I got another name for it,' grunted Sheriff Bush, staring at the tall Ranger with frank admiration.

Hatfield chuckled. He glanced at the window which was greying with the first light of dawn. Pinching out the butt of his cigarette, he stood up, smiling down at them from his great height.

'Well, I reckon that's about all,' he said. 'Releford's confession will give yuh all the evidence yuh need to convict the Death Riders, Sheriff. Sorry I can't stay on for the wedding, Teri, but Captain Bill has another little chore ready for me and I gotta trail my rope.'

They watched him ride away through a world all glorious with morning, tall and graceful atop his great golden horse, a pleased expression of anticipation in his strangely coloured eyes, to where duty called, and danger and new adventure waited.